The Plague of Thieves Affair

The Plague of Thieves Affair

A CARPENTER AND QUINCANNON MYSTERY

MARCIA MULLER

BILL PRONZINI

A TOM DOHERTY ASSOCIATES BOOK  NEW YORK

THE PLAGUE OF THIEVES AFFAIR

A Forge Book
Published by Tom Doherty Associates, LLC
175 Fifth Avenue
New York, NY 10010

www.tor-forge.com

Forge® is a registered trademark of Tom Doherty Associates, LLC.

The Library of Congress Cataloging-in-Publication Data
is available upon request.

ISBN 978-0-7653-8104-0 (hardcover)
ISBN 978-1-4668-7678-1 (e-book)

Our books may be purchased in bulk for promotional, educational, or business use. Please contact your local bookseller or the Macmillan Corporate and Premium Sales Department at (800) 221-7945, extension 5442, or by e-mail at MacmillanSpecialMarkets@macmillan.com.

First Edition: January 2016

Printed in the United States of America

0 9 8 7 6 5 4 3 2 1

For the folks at Tor/Forge, with our thanks
for giving Carpenter and Quincannon a good home

The Plague of Thieves Affair

1

QUINCANNON

There were few more undesirable places for a detective and committed temperance man to be plying his trade, John Quincannon reflected sourly, not for the first time in the past few days, than the bowels of a blasted brewery.

The fine, rich perfume of malt, hops, yeast, and brewing and fermenting beer permeated every nook and cranny of the two-story, block-square brick building that housed Golden State Steam Beer. Whenever he prowled its multitude of rooms and passages, he was enveloped in a pungent miasma that tightened his throat and dried his mouth, creating a thirst that plain water couldn't quite slake.

In his drinking days he had been mightily fond of the type of lager, invented during the Gold Rush and unique to San Francisco, known as "steam beer." John Wieland's Philadelphia Brewery, the National Brewery, and others operating in the city in this year of 1896 specialized in porter and pilsner; if one of their owners had sought the services of Carpenter and Quincannon, Professional Detective Services, he would not be suffering such pangs as this place instilled in him. But it had been Golden State's James Willard who had come calling, and the fee he'd offered for an investigation into the bizarre death of the head brewmaster, Otto Ackermann, was a sum no self-respecting Scot in his right mind could afford to turn down.

In the five years since Quincannon had taken the pledge, he had seldom been even mildly tempted to return to his bibulous ways. Even on his regular visits to his favorite watering hole, Hoolihan's Saloon on Second Street, to spend an evening with cronies or clients, he hadn't once considered imbibing anything stronger than his usual mug of clam juice. But after four days in Golden State's rarefied atmosphere, his craving for a tankard of San Francisco's best steam beer had grown to the barely manageable level. Another few days here and he might well be shamefully if briefly seduced.

Well, such a temporary fall should not be in the offing. He wouldn't be here in the guise of a city sanitation inspector for a second week, or even for one more day, if matters developed as he now believed they would. In anticipation of such a development, he wore his .36 Navy Colt holstered under his coat—the very same 1861 model sidearm his father had carried in the company of Allan Pinkerton during the Civil War, re-chambered now for metal cartridges. Until today, he had honored Willard's aversion to firearms and refusal to permit them in his brewery. Under the present circumstances, however, Quincannon had no qualms about ignoring his employer's edict; a detective on the verge of unmasking and arresting a dangerous felon was a fool to do so unarmed. The weapon, necessary or not, was a comfortably familiar weight on his hip.

Instead of entering the brewery with the arriving employees, as he had on previous mornings, he loitered outside the main entrance. The cold, fog-laden, late January wind was much preferable to the brewery perfume. He smoked a pipeful of navy cut tobacco, feigning interest in the big dray wagons with both full and empty kegs that emerged from the wagon entrance and rumbled past on Fremont Street.

He had been there some five minutes when James Willard arrived. The brewery owner paused for a moment as if thinking of having a word with Quincannon, rightly changed his mind—this was no place to discuss matters pertaining to an undercover investigation—and moved past with no more than a nod. His step was less than brisk, his back and shoulders bowed as if he bore an invisible weight. A large florid man of fifty-odd years, Willard had gray-flecked sideburns that resembled woolly tufts of cotton and morose gray eyes. A worry-prone gent even at the best of times. And with just cause under the present circumstances.

Otto Ackermann's death had shaken him badly, not only because the head brewmaster had been a trusted employee, but because it was Ackermann who had developed the formula for "the finest steam beer on the West Coast." It was his fear that Ackermann had not died in a freak accident, as the incompetent minions of the law had determined after a cursory investigation, but that he had been coshed and then pitched into the vat of fermenting beer to drown. And that the reason behind the murder was a plot to steal Ackermann's secret recipe. For no other local brewmaster had been able to equal the unique proportions in which the German immigrant mixed his ingredients, or the manner in which he treated them in the processing. Should a rival brewery manage to obtain the formula and begin brewing lager of comparable quality, Golden State's reputation would suffer and sales decline as a result.

Only one of Willard's competitors was cutthroat enough to collude in, if not sponsor, such a scheme—the small but aggressive West Star Brewing Company. Its owner, Cyrus Drinkwater (an ironic name for a beer mogul), was a morally bankrupt businessman who often used quasi-illegal if not downright illegal methods to make his fortune. He had his busy fingers in several pies, not the least of which was a silent partnership in the Gray Brothers Quarry Company—an outfit engaged in supplying crushed stone for construction and street and sidewalk paving, by systematically dynamiting the eastern face of Telegraph Hill and hillsides in Noe Valley. The Grays, George and Harry, were also notoriously unscrupulous. Their careless quarry blasting had crushed homes, destroyed lots, severely injured several people. Numerous lawsuits had been filed against them, to little or no avail; weak law enforcement and the city's corrupt political machine had permitted them to continue operating as they saw fit. Drinkwater, too, had escaped retribution and likewise operated with impunity in this and his other enterprises.

Quincannon had yet to tie Otto Ackermann's death to Drinkwater and West Star, but he was now tolerably sure that the brewmaster had in fact been a homicide victim, that he knew who had created what Willard referred to as a "devil's brew" in that vat of fermenting beer, and that the owner's fears of a plot to steal the master formula were justified. What was needed now was additional proof. Once he had that, he would collapse the entire scheme like the proverbial house of cards.

Ah, think of the devil and he appears. For here came his man now—Caleb Lansing, Golden State's assistant brewmaster.

Lansing, heavily bundled in cap, bandanna, and peacoat, barely glanced at him as he hurried into the building. Quincannon essayed a small satisfied smile round the stem of his briar. Lansing, he was sure, had no idea that he was under suspicion or of what lay ahead for him. Yaffling the man would be a pleasure, the more so because it would allow Quincannon to once again prove his long-held belief that he was a far better detective than any of those on the public payroll, most of whom couldn't be counted on to detect a horseshoe in a bowl of Irish stew.

When he finished his smoke, he knocked out the dottle on the sole of his boot and stored the briar in the pocket of his chesterfield. Then, instead of entering the brewery, he strolled briskly to Market Street where he boarded a westbound trolley car.

He rode the car as far as Duboce, walked two blocks south from there to Fourteenth Street—a workingman's neighborhood of beer halls, oyster dealers, Chinese laundries, grocers, and other small merchants. The front door of the nondescript boardinghouse where Lansing hung his hat was unlatched; Quincannon sauntered in as if he belonged there, climbed creaking stairs to the second floor.

The hallway there was deserted. He paused before the door bearing a pot-metal numeral 8 and tested the latch. Locked, naturally. Not that this presented a problem. Quincannon had developed certain skills during his years as an operative with the United States Secret Service and his subsequent time as a private investigator, some of which rivaled those of the most accomplished yeggs and housebreakers. The set of burglar tools he had liberated from a scruff named Wandering Ned several years ago, and which he now carried with him at all times in a small pouch, gave him swift access to Caleb Lansing's two small rooms.

Both sitting room and bedroom were as untidy as most bachelor's quarters, cluttered with personal items and several bottles of rye whiskey both empty and full. But no steam beer; Lansing evidently had little taste for what he helped brew. Quincannon commenced a methodical search, beginning with a moderately large steamer trunk at the foot of an unmade bed. It yielded naught but clothing and a faded daguerreotype of a plump young woman, scantily dressed, which was inscribed "To Caleb from his Sugar Sweet." Sugar Sweet. Faugh!

He found nothing of interest in the closet, the bureau, or anywhere else in the bedroom. His first important discovery came when he examined the fireplace. It was gas-fitted, its iron grate little more than a cheap ornament, but something had been burned there nonetheless. Caught around one of its legs was a partially charred note penned in a sprawling backhand. Some of the writing was still legible, including an injunction from the writer to Lansing to destroy it after reading. Also present was the writer's signature, the initials X.J. And damning this was, for very few men in San Francisco could lay claim to those initials. Quincannon knew of only one: Xavier Jones, the head brewmaster at West Star Brewing Company.

A smile parted his freebooter's whiskers as he tucked the paper carefully inside his billfold. Little doubt remained now that Cyrus Drinkwater had a hand in this dirty business.

His second find took longer, but was equally rewarding. In

a small strongbox cleverly (but not too cleverly) concealed beneath a loose floorboard he found a sheaf of greenbacks bound together with a rubber band and a handful of double eagles. A quick count revealed the total to be slightly more than two thousand dollars.

As much as he enjoyed the look and feel of spendable currency, he hesitated only a few seconds before returning the money to the strongbox and the strongbox to its hiding place. Only a corrupt detective would appropriate a wad of greenbacks, illegally obtained by Lansing though they were. John Frederick Quincannon was many things, but a thief was not one of them. He would inform the police of the booty and its whereabouts once Lansing was in their custody. Of course the cash might well mysteriously disappear before it could be used as evidence against Lansing in court—more than a few dicks on the city payroll lacked Quincannon's code of ethics— but that was not his concern. His duty was to himself, his reputation, and his clients, no more and no less.

His mouth quirked wryly as he straightened. Criminals— bah! The lot of them, fortunately, were arrogant and careless dolts. Lansing's failure to completely burn the note and his hiding of the payoff money here in his rooms, coupled with the testimony of the witness Quincannon had found who'd seen him entering the brewery late on the night of Otto Ackermann's murder and Lansing's bald denial of this fact, was more than sufficient evidence to arrest him and eventually help hang him.

Quincannon whistled an old temperance tune, "The Brewers' Big Horses Can't Run Over Me," as he relocked the door to the assistant brewmaster's rooms and then left the boardinghouse. Naught was left but to confront Lansing, urge a confession out of him through one means or another, then hand him over to those blue-coated denizens of the Hall who had the audacity to call themselves San Francisco's finest. Then he could collect his fee from James Willard, and return to the relative peace and clean, brewery-free air of Carpenter and Quincannon, Professional Detective Services.

Where only one temptation awaited him—one he would succumb to in an instant were the opportunity to present itself. A possibility, by Godfrey, that was not as unlikely as it had once seemed, not for a man as determined and optimistic as John Frederick Quincannon. For in the words of Emily Dickinson, one of his favorite poets, "Hope is the thing with feathers / That perches in the soul."

Ah, Sabina. Dear Sabina.

2

SABINA

Sabina entertained three visitors that morning in the Market Street offices of Carpenter and Quincannon, Professional Detective Services. The first two arrived together to confirm their hiring of the agency for what promised to be a routine matter, though one of some interest to her. The third individual was a complete stranger, and who he was and what he wanted came as a startling surprise.

Marcel Carreaux and Andrew Rayburn, the first two callers, arrived promptly for their ten o'clock appointment. Both were well dressed in the fashion of the day—sack coats with covered buttons and matching waistcoats, gray and dark brown respectively; stiff-collared shirts, bow ties, narrow-brimmed bowler hats—but otherwise they were as unalike as two gentlemen could be. Their only commonality, so far as Sabina knew, was an abiding love of artistic creation in its many forms.

Carreaux, tall, spare, with ascetic features and elegantly tonsured silver hair, was assistant curator of the Louvre Museum in Paris; the short, balding, fussy Rayburn, whose most prominent features were a large hooked nose and a thin shoelace mustache, owned the well-regarded Rayburn Art Gallery on Post Street. The Frenchman bowed formally, said, "*Enchanté, madame,*" and when she gave him her hand, actually bestowed a brief Gallic kiss on the back of her hand. The gallery owner, whom she had met before, favored her with a professional smile as skimpy as his mustache.

What had brought the two men together was an exhibition of rare and valuable antique ladies' handbags, dubbed Reticules Through the Ages, which had just arrived under railroad guard from Seattle, its previous stop on a nationwide, twelve-city American tour; the exhibit was due to open for public viewing at the Rayburn Gallery two days hence. It was on Andrew Rayburn's recommendation that Carpenter and Quincannon, Professional Detective Services, be hired to provide security for the week-long showing in San Francisco. Sabina's only communication with Carreaux had been an exchange of wires during his stay in Seattle.

"We have had no difficulties in other cities, Madame Carpenter, nor do we expect any here," the Frenchman said when he and Rayburn were seated before her desk. "*Mais non.* But San Francisco is known to be, ah, a city in which there is much wickedness . . ."

"Deservedly so," Rayburn said in his fussy way. "Thieves abound in the Barbary Coast. Criminals who will steal anything of value if they can, anything at all. The district is a blight on our fair escutcheon."

"Thus it is better to be safe than sorry, *n'est-ce pas?*"

"The Marie Antoinette chatelaine bag alone is valued at several thousand dollars," Rayburn added. He smoothed his rather silly little mustache with a neatly manicured forefinger.

"It and the other items must be protected while they are on display in my gallery."

"At all times, m'sieu *et* madame, and in all places until their safe return to Paris."

"Yes, of course, but especially here."

Sabina said, "The Marie Antoinette bag is the centerpiece of the exhibition, I gather."

Carreaux gave an enthusiastic nod of agreement. "A true treasure—*c'est magnifique!*"

He went on to explain that in olden times, chatelaine bags had hung from an ornamental hook on the jeweled girdles of ladies of high station and contained useful household items—a fact Sabina already knew. Made of beadwork or silver or gold mesh, many were set with precious or semiprecious gems. The Marie Antoinette was one of these. Six by ten inches in size, it was fashioned of pure gold mesh, its rigid gold frame and clasp encrusted with diamonds and rubies.

Such a history it had! The Queen of France and Navarre had worn it at Versailles. Along with many other valuables, it had been seized by French revolutionists after the kingdom fell in 1792, and she and the rest of the royal family were imprisoned (and eventually executed), and paraded through the streets of Paris as an example of the monarchy's profligate ways. For two decades afterward it was believed to have been lost or destroyed. Ah, but then it had resurfaced in the possession of a descendant of a minor revolutionary, who donated it to the Louvre Museum where it had been repaired and restored. And there it had been permanently displayed until M. Bernard La Follette, curator, joined with curators from museums in Florence and Venice to bring it and some two dozen other historically significant European handbags to America under his, Marcel Carreaux's, guidance.

Private galleries in each city on the tour had been chosen to display Reticules Through the Ages, rather than museums or exhibition halls. One reason was that the collection was small and required relatively little space for viewing, but security was the primary factor. It was much easier to provide safeguards in a gallery venue, where entrances and exits were few and there were no dark nooks and crannies that could be used as hiding places. The Rayburn Art Gallery, which Sabina had visited, had been an excellent choice for both viewing and security purposes here. It was prominently located, and while Reticules Through the Ages would be open to the general public, the audience would consist primarily of members of the city's social elite to whom invitations had been issued. The assignment promised to be a simple one and Sabina had been glad to accept it. The opportunity to view such a splendid collection of historical artifacts was a pleasure she looked forward to, and even John would agree that the fee was excellent.

"As I indicated during our previous meeting," Rayburn said, "the exhibit will be open during evening hours only, from five until nine o'clock. How many men will you supply, Mrs. Carpenter? Properly attired, of course."

"None."

"How's that? None?"

"I'll attend to the duties myself."

He blinked at her owlishly. "With no male assistance?"

Sabina bit back a sharp retort. The man was something of a pompous, self-serving ass and she would have liked to tell him so, but it would never do for the watchdog to bite the hand that was feeding it. She said only, "One guard should be sufficient, and I assure you I am quite competent," and then turned her attention to the Frenchman. "I trust you have no objection to my giving this matter my personal attention, Mr. Carreaux."

"I have heard only praise of your abilities, not only from M'sieu Rayburn but others as well. *Mais oui*, I am quite comfortable with the arrangement you suggest."

"Well, if you are, Marcel, then so am I," Rayburn said, though he didn't sound convinced. He gave his mustache another fussy stroking. "Though I still think the presence of two detectives is preferable to one."

"At twice the fee per evening," Sabina reminded him.

A tendency toward penny-pinching evidently was another of the gallery owner's less than endearing qualities. He made no further protest, saying only, "Mm, yes, well," in a vague sort of way.

A signed contract and a retainer check concluded the arrangements. Sabina promised to present herself at the Rayburn Gallery at four P.M. the following afternoon, one hour before the grand opening, and the two men took their leave, M. Carreaux once again gallantly bowing and bestowing a kiss on her hand. A courtly and quite likable man. The opposite of Andrew Rayburn in that respect, too.

Alone at her desk, busy with routine paperwork, she found herself wondering how John was faring with his investigation into the death of Golden State Steam Beer's brewmaster. As usual, her partner had been reticent about discussing a case in progress, but from his good humor yesterday afternoon she presumed that he was close to a satisfactory resolution. Well, in any event it was fortunate that just a single operative, her, would be providing security for Reticules Through the Ages. Even if John were free on any of the evenings, he would have protested vehemently against joining her at the Rayburn gallery. She could just hear his response if it were suggested to him. "Handbags! Reticules! Bah!" Had M. Carreaux and Andrew Rayburn insisted that a male operative also be present, she would've had to bring in one of the agency's part-time operatives.

Still, she found herself picturing John in evening clothes, as she'd seen him wear on a few previous occasions. With his broad shoulders and luxuriant beard, he cut a handsome figure in both a dark tailcoat, striped trousers, and ruffled shirt, and a dinner jacket with a shawl collar and silk facings. As handsome a figure, she admitted on reflection, as Carson Montgomery had presented during their brief relationship.

Carson. She hadn't seen him since they had said good-bye outside the Palace Hotel last October, after she'd confronted him with her discoveries about his somewhat checkered past. Nor had he attempted to contact her. Fortunately they didn't travel in the same social circles; it might have been awkward if their paths had happened to cross. She wished him the best, but thought of him less and less and had no regrets that their brief liaison failed to develop along more intimate lines.

Her time with him, however, had wrought a certain change in her, perhaps even a profound change—one that might be labeled "Not Enough." One of the traits that her late husband, Stephen, had most valued in her was her flexibility, her capacity for dealing with life's adversities and then moving forward. He would have understood, though not approved, of her temporary plunge into depression after the outlaw's bullet took his life, but he would have been proud when she'd finally dragged herself out of the depths and plunged back into her work as a Pink Rose. And he would have applauded, she was sure, her move to San Francisco, her partnership with John, and her new life here.

But while that new life had been fulfilling, it no longer seemed to be complete enough. Much as she enjoyed her friendships with women she'd met through her cousin Callie French, much as she loved her cats, Adam and Eve, they were not adequate substitutes for meaningful male companionship. The interlude with Carson had reminded her that she was a healthy, attractive woman in the prime of life; that she did not have to remain a celibate widow for the rest of her days. Nor would Stephen have wanted her to. Sometimes when she viewed the cats as they played or slept curled together, she thought: *They have each other. Whom do I have?*

Well, she could have John if she chose. He had made it plain from the beginning that he yearned for a personal relationship, but she had been convinced that his motive was nothing more than seduction, despite his protestations to the contrary. For that reason, and because of the pain of Stephen's loss, she'd kept him firmly at arm's length. As she'd kept all other men at arm's length before Carson. Lately, however, she had begun to think that John's feelings for her as a woman went well beyond mere sexual conquest.

For five years now she had steadfastly maintained, to him and to herself, that a personal relationship would not mix with the professional. But wasn't that merely an excuse to avoid intimacy? She and Stephen had shared both in Chicago and in

Denver, with no adverse effects on their work or their marriage; if anything, the sharing had made their bond stronger. Of course Stephen had been the love of her life; she could never love another as deeply. Still, and she might as well admit it, what she had come to feel for John was something more than just a sisterly affection.

He was an attractive man, no question of that. A good man, too, with a keen intelligence and a strong moral sense beneath his occasionally reckless and acquisitive behavior. He could be pompous, moody, critical, but more often he was kind and courtly and jocular; inside his crusty shell, she suspected, he was as soft and perhaps as sweet as custard. Stephen had been a gentle, considerate, doting husband and lover. Despite John's faults, wasn't it possible he would be the same?

Not Enough.

She had already weakened to the point of allowing an occasional social evening's entertainment, and he had been a perfect gentleman on each occasion; had not even once attempted to kiss her. Should she give him even more of a chance to prove himself? Not by succumbing to him physically—she was still not ready for that degree of intimacy—but by allowing him to spark her as a prospective beau would. The thought was appealing, yet she still felt reluctant. Her hands-off demeanor was her defense against a world that might brutally hurt her again. What if she were to become romantically involved with John, a risk-taking man in the same dangerous profession as Stephen, and something happened to him, too? She was a strong woman, but not strong enough, she feared, to survive a second painful loss . . .

Her reverie was interrupted, perhaps fortunately, by the

arrival of the morning's third visitor. He entered after a rather loud knock, apparently made with the silver hound's-head knob on the walking stick he carried—a slim, fair-haired young man whom she had never seen before. He stood for a moment after closing the door, wrinkled his nose as if in disapproval of the surroundings, and then approached Sabina's desk as she rose to her feet.

His disapproval didn't extend to her; his roving gaze and rather rakish smile attested to that. A gay blade, she thought. And a dandified one, dressed in an expensive dove-gray sack coat, floral waistcoat, striped trousers, orange silk cravat, and high-topped leather shoes polished to a gloss. A diamond stickpin in his cravat gave off an opulent dazzle—a little too much dazzle, Sabina thought, for the stone to be genuine. His pale hair was cut short, parted in the middle and slicked down, and his chin was adorned with a small pointed beard.

"Do I have the pleasure of addressing Mrs. Sabina Carpenter?"

"You do. And you are, sir?"

"Roland W. Fairchild. Of Chicago, Illinois."

He presented her with a gold-embossed card, which told her nothing more than he just had except for the fact that he was an attorney-at-law. She invited him to sit down, waited until he did so before reseating herself. He sat erect with his knees together, the stick propped between them, and smiled—half leered—at her across the desk.

"A lady detective, and a most attractive one," he said. "Such an interesting novelty."

Sabina had already begun to dislike Roland W. Fairchild of Chicago, Illinois; that silly comment firmed her opinion. She didn't respond to it, instead adopted a stern, no-nonsense look to show him what she thought of it and his overly bold appraisal of her.

"What can I do for you, Mr. Fairchild?"

"I should like to engage you to find a missing person."

"One of our specialties," she said, stretching the truth a trifle. "The name of this person?"

"Charles Percival Fairchild the Third. My first cousin."

"Also of Chicago?"

"Originally."

"How long has he been missing?"

"From his last known address, approximately seventeen months. I myself haven't seen him in more than three years."

"Seventeen months? That's quite a long time, Mr. Fairchild. Were you only recently made aware of his absence?"

"No. We—that is, the family—have known of it for some time. It only became necessary to make a concerted effort to locate him when his father, Charles P. Fairchild the Second, the noted industrialist, died recently." The aquiline nose twitched again. "My cousin is sole heir to the estate."

"I see. Are you the deceased Mr. Fairchild's attorney?"

"For the estate? No. Merely an emissary acting on their behalf as a member of the family."

"You have reason to believe your cousin is in San Francisco?"

"That he was here, yes, and hope still is. If so, you and your partner, Mr. Quincannon, are uniquely qualified to locate him."

"Uniquely qualified? I don't understand."

"You have had business dealings with Charles before, so I've been reliably informed. On more than one occasion."

"I'm afraid I don't recall a client named Charles Fairchild—"

"He was not a client. And you know him by a different name." Still another nose twitch. Roland Fairchild then withdrew a photograph from an inside pocket of his sack coat, reached across the desk to lay it faceup in front of Sabina. "Charles is the poor daft chap who fancies himself to be the late British detective Sherlock Holmes."

3

SABINA

Sabina was, to put it mildly, taken aback. And temporarily rendered mute. She realized her jaw had hinged open, closed her mouth, and sat staring down at the photograph.

It appeared to be a professional head-and-shoulders portrait taken sometime within the past five years, and the likeness was unmistakable. The lean, hawklike face and piercing eyes that peered up at her was in fact the bogus Sherlock—bogus Englishman, too, evidently—who had during the previous year insinuated himself into three cases of hers and John's with rather amazing results; who had a conjurer's habit of appearing and disappearing at will; who possessed an uncanny knack for ferreting out information about all sorts of goings-on in San Francisco's underworld; who drove John to distraction and bewildered and irritated her, yet had demonstrated a surprising kindliness the last time she saw him by presenting her with the kitten she'd named Eve.

She found her voice. "My Lord," she said. "Sherlock Holmes."

"Ah. You do recognize him, then."

"Yes. Oh, yes."

"Do you know his present whereabouts?"

"No. Neither my partner nor I have seen or heard from him since last October."

"If he is still lurking about San Francisco, have you any idea where he might be found?"

She shook her head. "His last known address was the Old Union Hotel on Geary Street, but that was several months ago. And he lodged there only a short time."

"Do you think you could manage to track him down, wherever he might be now?"

"I don't know. Possibly."

"Would you make the effort for a mutually agreeable fee?"

Sabina stared down at the photograph again. Charles Percival Fairchild III. The name certainly suited the man, though it would be a while before she thought of him as other than the self-proclaimed Mr. Holmes. "He is heir to his late father's estate, you said?"

"Sole heir. Quite a substantial estate it is, too. My uncle amassed a fortune in Chicago's meatpacking industry." Roland Fairchild leaned forward confidentially. "Cousin Charles stands to inherit slightly more than three million dollars."

If John had been present, he might well have whistled at the amount. Sabina managed not to blink.

"That is, of course," Fairchild said, "if he can be found, is willing to return to Chicago, and once there, is not judged incompetent by a court-appointed alienist."

"And if he were? Would you stand to inherit in his stead?"

The young dandy's smile quirked at the corners. "You mustn't think I have ulterior motives, Mrs. Carpenter."

"I have no such thoughts," Sabina fibbed. "I was merely asking a question."

"The answer to which is yes."

"Do you believe he's incompetent?"

"Well, a man who has assumed the identity of a rather famous and deceased individual can hardly be considered sane, can he?" Nose twitch. "Charles always was a bit queer. Quite intelligent, well read, well spoken, but nonetheless lacking in mental stability."

"How did he become obsessed with Sherlock Holmes? Do you know?"

"Specifically, no. My uncle sent him to England when he was in his early twenties, to be educated at Oxford. Our family has British forebears, you see. Charles the Second's father was born in England."

"Did he complete his studies there?"

"Yes, with honors. And developed into a confirmed Anglophile in the process. He came home to Chicago for a time, at my uncle's urging, but then skipped off again to England." Twitch. "A generous monthly stipend, overly generous to my way of thinking, allowed him to live quite well in London."

"Where he was exposed to the genuine Holmes's exploits and grew to admire him to an irrational degree."

"Yes. He also bears a physical resemblance to the genuine article, I understand. He wrote of this in one of his early letters, claiming the resemblance to be so uncanny that they might have been twins."

"He made no secret of his obsession, then?"

"On the contrary. He reveled in it. Though at first it seemed more a case of uncontrolled hero worship than actual impersonation."

"When did he come to believe that he was Holmes? Was it when the detective died in Switzerland?"

"That may well have been what tipped him over. In his last letter, more than two years ago, he wrote that rumors of 'his' alleged death were false and 'he' was very much alive and intended to continue 'his' inquiries, as he called them, elsewhere. He signed it 'S. Holmes, Esquire.'"

"What did his father think of this?"

"He was upset, of course. He sought to bring Charles back to Chicago for treatment by an alienist, but his letters and cables went unanswered. The old gentleman's health was too poor to permit him to travel to England. Through his attorneys he hired investigators in London, but they found no trace of Charles there or anywhere else. He simply disappeared."

"Did he indicate in his last letter that he might travel to San Francisco?"

"No," Fairchild said. "It was only after my uncle's death that we—the attorneys for the estate and I, that is—discovered that Charles had come here and was posing as Holmes."

"How did you find out?"

"By happenstance. My uncle's law firm is one of Chicago's largest and they have had dealings with a San Francisco firm—Stennett, Tyler, and Dubois. Perhaps you've heard of them?"

Sabina nodded. They were respected corporate attorneys.

"Harold Stennett was in Chicago on a business matter," Fairchild said. "He met with my uncle's attorney, Leland Hazelton, and chanced to mention that a man claiming to be

Holmes had been involved in a rather sensational murder case with a pair of genuine private investigators. Mr. Stennett provided your and your partner's names. He also offered to contact your firm upon his return, but Mr. Hazelton and I decided it would be best if I undertook the task myself. In the event Charles is found, I stand a better chance than anyone else of convincing him to return to Chicago. As a member of the family and because we have always had a reasonably cordial relationship."

"I see. Is there anything else I should know?"

"I don't believe so. You'll conduct a search, then? Or will you need to consult with your partner before committing?"

"That won't be necessary," Sabina said, having no intention of doing so. She had been taking notes; she laid down her fountain pen, brushed a stray wisp of her seal-black hair off her forehead, and sat back. "You may rest assured every effort will be made to locate your cousin wherever he may be. There are no guarantees, of course."

"Will you be able to begin immediately?"

"I don't see why not."

"And how will you go about it?"

"Our methods are private by necessity, as I'm sure you can understand. But you have my assurance that you will be immediately notified of any pertinent developments."

"That is satisfactory. What are your fees?"

She named a retainer figure, an amount somewhat less than John surely would have asked.

"Also satisfactory. Shall I write you a check now?"

"If you like." But she wouldn't deposit it in the agency account until she checked to make absolutely sure Roland W. Fairchild was who and what he claimed to be.

While he was writing the check with a gold fountain pen of his own, Sabina asked, "Where can you be reached, Mr. Fairchild?"

"We have a suite at the Baldwin Hotel."

"We?"

"My wife Octavia and I. Like me, she has always longed to visit the 'Paris of America' and all its charming attractions."

Fairchild's smile turned wistful as he spoke, as if he secretly wished he'd come alone to the "Paris of America"—a city as famous for its sinful attractions as for its charming ones. A roving-eyed gay blade like Roland Fairchild, if he were here untethered and unsupervised, would have had himself a grand time in the flesh palaces and gambling halls of the Barbary Coast and Uptown Tenderloin. His wife must be a forceful woman, and a perceptive one, to have convinced him to bring her with him.

Sabina said, keeping her voice free of irony, "I hope you'll both enjoy the many available pleasures during your stay."

"I'm sure we will." Fairchild stood. "And I hope I shall hear from you soon with positive news."

"Soon in any case, Mr. Fairchild. Good day."

A reply in kind, followed by another small raffish smile, and he was gone. The strong scent of his bay rum remained, however; Sabina opened the window facing on Market Street to let in breaths of cold fresh air.

Had she been a little too hasty in accepting his proposition and his check? Not because of her dislike of the dandified

Mr. Roland Fairchild, and not because she doubted her ability to locate his delusional cousin if such were possible; the undertaking was worthwhile if only to give Charles Percival Fairchild III the option of returning to Chicago to attempt to claim his inheritance. No, the concern lay in the prospect of dealing with him again in his vainglorious and vaguely sinister Sherlock Holmes role.

Their last meeting had been an amicable one, but his secretive involvement with Carson Montgomery's past and present troubles had left her with further doubts about his sanity. There was no question that he was shrewd and his deductive powers considerable—he had proved that on more than one occasion—but last October he'd given her reason to suspect that his methods were not quite as cerebral and nonviolent as those of the genuine Mr. Holmes. She wasn't afraid of him, but her uncertainty as to the exact nature of his instability was unsettling.

John had similar feelings, though for different reasons. Sabina hadn't told him about the unpleasant business with Carson; it would have served no good purpose. His aversion to "Holmes" was motivated by enmity and jealousy, the poseur having dealt a blow to John's self-esteem during their investigation of the Bughouse Affair. As far as he knew, the thorn in his side had been plucked out for good the previous summer, after the close of the Spook Lights Affair. Should she tell him of the crackbrain's true identity and what the present assignment entailed? He was entitled to know, of course, but it would probably make him furious. No, not probably—definitely. The best course, then, was to proceed privately with the search for Charles Percival Fairchild III; and however it turned out, to give John an ex post facto explanation. His feathers wouldn't be quite so ruffled then, especially if her investigation resulted in Charles the Third's departure for a city two thousand miles from San Francisco.

Having settled this in her mind, Sabina turned her thoughts to the task itself. How would she go about tracking down a man who never remained long in one place, who was prone to adopting outlandish disguises, and who seemed to thrive on shadowy associations with thieves, blackmailers, and other crooks?

Three starting points occurred to her, one direct, two indirect. The latter pair were the most likely to succeed, but both required an unknown amount of passive waiting. The direct one first, then. But not until she had verification of Roland W. Fairchild's bona fides.

She pinned on her new straw boater with its stylish trim of ostrich tips and crushed ribbons (inelegantly referred to as a "settin' hen" by some), donned her fur-collared long coat, locked the office, and set off on her rounds.

4

QUINCANNON

Golden State's business offices were clustered at the east end of the second floor, all of them small and cramped except for the two-room office inhabited by James Willard. This was Quincannon's first stop upon his return to the brewery, but Willard was not there. His secretary said he had left to attend a meeting and hadn't been sure when he would be back.

Quincannon debated. Should he wait to relay his information to the brewery owner before bracing Caleb Lansing? No, he decided. He was a patient man most of the time, but not when he was about to put the arm on a lawbreaker. He didn't need Willard's blessings to make a citizen's arrest, and the sooner Lansing was in his custody the better.

He strode down the hall to the assistant brewmaster's cubicle, found it empty, and proceeded to the nearest occupied space, that of the company bookkeeper and paymaster, Elias Corby. He poked his head inside and asked, "Would you know where I can find Caleb Lansing, Mr. Corby?"

Corby, a pint-sized, long-nosed gent dressed in striped

galluses and rough twill trousers, paused in his writing in an open ledger book. "Lansing? Why, no, I don't."

"When did you see him last?"

"Just after I arrived this morning. Have you tried the brewhouse?"

"My next stop."

The brewhouse was at the opposite end of the building. Lansing was nowhere to be found in the rooms containing the malt storage tanks and mash tun. Jacob Drew, the mash boss, a red-haired, red-bearded giant, reported that he'd seen the assistant brewmaster in the fermenting room a few minutes earlier.

"What d'ye want with him, mister?" Drew asked. "Something to do with your inspections?"

"You might say that."

"The lad's a weak stick, but he's done competent enough work since poor Ackermann's accident."

"Work, yes," Quincannon said, "though not in the brewer's art."

He left Drew looking puzzled and followed a sinuous maze of piping to the fermenting room, a cavernous space filled with gas-fired cookers and cedar-wood fermenting tanks some nine feet in height and circumference. Two of the cookers contained bubbling wort, an oatmeal-like mixture of water, mashed barley, and soluble starch turned into fermentable sugar during the mashing process. After the wort was hopped and brewed, it would be filtered and fermented to produce "steam beer"— a term that had nothing to do with the use of actual steam. The lager was made with bottom-fermenting yeast at sixty to seventy degrees Fahrenheit, rather than the much lower temperatures necessary for true lager fermentation, because the city's winters were never cold enough to reach the freezing point. Additional keg fermentation resulted in a blast of foam and the loud hiss of escaping carbon dioxide when the kegs were tapped, a sound not unlike the release of a steam boiler's valve.

The heady aroma was strongest here. Once again Quincannon's nostrils began to quiver, his mouth and throat to feel like the inside of a corroded drainpipe. He had the fanciful, and rueful, wish that a man could be fitted with a relief valve as easily as a boiler, to ease pressure buildup inside his head.

On the catwalk above the cookers, Caleb Lansing stood supervising the adding of dried hops to the cooking wort. Workmen with long-handled wooden paddles stirred the mixture, while others skimmed off the dark, lumpy scum called krausen, a blend of hop, resin, yeast, and impurities that rose to the surface. The slab floor, supported by heavy steel girders, was slick with globs of foam that a hose man sluiced at intervals into the drains.

Lansing was a rumpled, obsequious individual in his middle years, given to smoking odiferous short-sixes; cigar ash littered his loose-hanging vest and shirtfront. He had just finished consulting a turnip watch when he spied Quincannon. He'd been on his guard every time they'd met previously, even though he had little to fear from a man he believed to be no more than a city inspector. Now, nervous tension once again pulled his vulpine features out of shape—the look of a guilty man. Quincannon had seen that look often enough to know it well.

Lansing swung away from the low railing, came forward as he approached, and sought to push past him. Quincannon blocked his way. "I'll have a word with you in private, Lansing."

"Not now you won't. Can't you see I'm busy?"

"My business with you won't wait."

"What business?"

"Otto Ackermann. Xavier Jones. Cyrus Drinkwater and West Star Brewing."

Fright shone in the assistant brewmaster's narrow face. "I don't know what you're talking about."

"The game's up, Lansing. I know the whole lay."

"You know . . . You're not an inspector. Who the devil are you?"

"I'll give you one guess."

Lansing muttered, "Dirty flycop!" under his breath and succeeded this time in shoving past him. He would have run then, but Quincannon grabbed the trailing flap of his vest and yanked him around.

"Come along and don't give me any trouble—"

The blasted rascal was quick as a cat, not with his hands but with his feet. The toe of his heavy work shoe thudded painfully into Quincannon's shin, broke his hold on the vest, and sent him reeling backward against the railing. Lansing spun and fled to the stairs before Quincannon, growling an oath, could regain his balance and stumble in pursuit.

Drawing his Navy Colt was out of the question; he couldn't very well fire it in these crowded confines, even in warning, and brandishing it would likely cause panic among the workers below. Instead he shouted as he clambered down the stairs, "Stop him! Stop that man!"

"No, no, don't let him catch me!" Lansing cried in return. "He's a madman, he's trying to kill me!"

The workers stood in clustered confusion, looking from one to the other of the running men. Lansing threaded through them, vaulted an intestinal coiling of pipes, and disappeared behind one of the vats. Quincannon might have snagged him before he escaped from the fermenting room if a mustached workman hadn't stepped into his path, saying, "Here, what's the idea of—*ufff!*" Quincannon bowled him over, but in doing so his foot slipped on the wet floor and he went skidding headfirst into a snakelike tangle of hose. By the time he disengaged himself and regained his feet, fought off clutching hands, and plunged ahead in a limping run, Lansing was nowhere to be seen.

There was only one way out of this section of the brewery. Still somewhat hobbled, Quincannon went through the boiler room, past the corner room where the vats of rejected beer stood in heavy shadow, then past the freight elevator and down the stairs to the lower floor. An electrically lit passage led into the main tunnel that divided the building in half. He hurried along the tunnel, out onto the Seventh Street loading dock. There was no sign of Lansing anywhere in the vicinity. Half a dozen burly workmen were wrestling filled kegs onto a pair of massive Studebaker wagons; Quincannon called to them. No, they hadn't seen Lansing come out.

So his quarry was still in the building. But for how long?

Quincannon's shin still smarted, but he could move more or less normally again; he ran back inside. Perpendicular to the tunnel was another wide corridor that led in one direction to the shipping offices and the main entrance, in the other to the cellars. There being no exit from the cellars, he hastened the other way. But almost immediately he encountered a clerk headed to the dock with a handful of bills of lading, who told him Lansing hadn't gone that way, either. The clerk had been conversing with another man in the passage for the past three or four minutes and would have seen him if he had.

Now Quincannon was nonplussed. He retraced his path along the side corridor to the brick-walled one that led downward to the cellars. A workman pushing a hand truck laden with fifty-pound sacks of barley was on his way up.

"Mr. Lansing? Yes, sir, just a few moments ago. Heading into the storerooms."

"The storerooms? Are you certain, man?"

"Aye. In a great hurry he was."

Why the devil would Lansing go there? To hide? Fool's game, if that was his intention. The storerooms, where all the ingredients that went into the mass production of beer were kept, were a collective dead end. So were the cellar rooms that housed filled kegs and the enormous cedar vats where "green" beer was ripened and finished beer was held before being piped to the company's bottling plant in a separate building adjacent.

Quincannon made his way down the passage, quickly but watchfully. The temperature dropped by several degrees as he descended. When he reached the artery that led to the storerooms, the air was frosty enough to require the buttoning of his coat—though he didn't do so, for it would have impeded access to the Navy Colt. He passed through a large room stacked on two sides with empty kegs. At its far end, a solid oak door barred the way into the remaining storerooms.

The door, Quincannon had been told, had been installed

as a deterrent to both rodents and human pilferage. Years before, a former brewery employee had returned late at night and helped himself to a wagonload of sugar and barley, and Willard would brook no repeat of that criminal business. The door was kept open during the day but locked at the end of shift. Only a handful of men in supervisory positions had keys.

It should not have been closed now. Nor should it have been locked, though it was. Quincannon muttered an imprecation. Lansing must have done the locking; he had access to a key. But why? What could he be up to back there?

Quincannon listened at the door. No sounds came to him through the heavy wood. He bent at the waist to peer through the keyhole. All he could make out was an empty section of concrete floor, weakly lighted by electric bulbs and shadow-ridden. He straightened again, scowling, tugging at his beard. The loading-dock foreman, Jack Malloy, would have a key. Find him, then, and waste no time doing so.

Just as he turned away, a muffled report sounded from somewhere behind the locked door. One he'd heard all too often to mistake for anything but what it was—a pistol shot.

Hell and damn! Quincannon swung back to the door, coming up hard against it, rattling it in its frame. Reflex made him tug futilely at the handle. No second report came, but when he pressed an ear to the wood he heard several faint sounds. Movement, but what sort he couldn't tell.

The silence that followed crackled with tension.

He pushed away again, ran back along the passage until he came upon a workman just emerging from the cellars. He sent the man after the loading-dock foreman, then took himself back to the storeroom door. He tested the latch to determine that it was still locked, though there was no way Lansing or anyone else could have come out and gotten past him.

Malloy arrived on the run, two other men trailing behind him. "What's the trouble here?" he demanded.

"Someone fired a pistol behind that locked door," Quincannon told him, "not five minutes ago."

"A pistol?" Malloy said, astonished. "In the storerooms?"

"I heard it plainly."

"But . . . why? How? Mr. Willard has strict orders against firearms on the premises . . ."

Quincannon made an impatient growling noise. "Button your lip, lad, and unlock the blasted door."

The foreman was used to the voice of authority; quickly he produced his ring of keys. The door opened inward and Quincannon crowded through first, his hand inside his coat and resting on the Navy's walnut handle. Two large, chilly rooms opened off the passage, one filled with sacks of barley, the other with boxes of yeast and fifty-pound sacks of malt, hops, and sugar stacked on end. Both enclosures were empty. The boxes and sacks were so tightly packed together that no one could have hidden behind or among them without being seen at a glance.

At the far end of the passage stood another closed door. "What's beyond there?" he asked the foreman.

"Utility room. Well pump and equipment storage."

Quincannon tried the door. It refused his hand on the latch. "You have a key, Malloy?"

"The lock's the same as on the outer door."

"Then open it, man, open it."

Malloy obeyed. The heavy, dank odors of mold and earth mingled with the acrid scent of gunpowder tickled Quincannon's nostrils as the door creaked inward. Only one electric bulb burned here. Gloom lay thick beyond the threshold, enfolding the shapes of well pump, coiled hoses, hand trucks, and other equipment. Quincannon produced a lucifer from his pocket, scraped it alight on the rough brick wall.

"Lord save us!" Malloy said.

Caleb Lansing lay sprawled on the dirt floor in front of the well pump. Blood glistened blackly on his shirt. Beside one outflung hand was an old LeMat revolver, the type that used pinfire cartridges. Loosely clenched in the other hand was the same type of brass key Malloy had used.

Quincannon knelt to press fingers against the artery in Lansing's neck. Not even the flicker of a pulse. No blackened powder burns rimmed the bloody wound under the left armpit.

"What are you men doing here? What's going on?"

The new voice belonged to Elias Corby, the long-nosed little bookkeeper. He pushed his way forward, sucked in his breath audibly when he saw what lay at his feet.

"Mr. Lansing's killed himself," Malloy said.

"Killed himself? Here?"

"Crazy place for it, by all that's holy."

"But why? Why would he do such a thing?"

"God only knows."

"Suicide," Corby said in awed tones. "Lansing, of all people."

Quincannon paid no attention to them. While they were gabbing, he finished his examination of the dead man and then picked up the LeMat revolver, hefted it, put it down again in the same place next to Lansing's hand.

Suicide?

Bah!

Murder, plain enough. Cold-blooded murder.

5

QUINCANNON

Quincannon kept his suspicions to himself. He was tolerably certain that a hand other than Caleb Lansing's had taken the man's life, for four good reasons, but he needed more time to determine the who, how, and why of the deed. Proclaiming here and now that Lansing had not died alone behind not one but two locked doors, the outer one under Quincannon's own surveillance, would have brought him scorn. Not to mention stirred the already boiling pot even more by adding unnecessary complications, and even more importantly, perhaps warned the scoundrel responsible for the crime.

He ordered Jack Malloy to relock the storeroom doors and stand guard, sent Elias Corby to summon the law, and rode the freight elevator back upstairs in the hope that James Willard had returned from his meeting. A few minutes with his client before the police arrived, to explain Lansing's involvement with the murder of Otto Ackermann to his client, would have prepared him for the interrogation to come. But Willard hadn't yet returned. Until he did, Quincannon would have to bear the brunt of the questioning.

He took himself downstairs to the brick-walled corridor leading to the cellars. A gaggle of workers had clustered there, drawn by fast-spread word of the shooting; he pushed his way through them to join the grim-faced Malloy. The two of them waited together in silence, the only sounds in the dank passage the muttering voices of the gathered men.

The wait lasted no more than ten minutes, a fast response for a change by an "ace detective" from the Hall of Justice. Quincannon's hope was that the officer in charge would be one he didn't know or knew only slightly, but he had no such luck. In fact, the man leading the half-dozen coppers who arrived on the scene was the one he least wanted to see—the beefy, red-faced Prussian named Kleinhoffer with whom he'd had run-ins in the past. Kleinhoffer was an incompetent political toady with dubious morals and a strong dislike of private detectives. His opinion of Quincannon was on a par with Quincannon's opinion of him.

When the dick spied him, his color darkened and his beady eyes and thin mouth pinched into a glower. "You, Quincannon. What the devil are you doing here?"

"Plying my trade, same as you."

"He's been here the past few days," Malloy said.

"Has he now. Doing what, exactly?"

"Inspecting the premises. He's a safety inspector for the Department of Public Works . . . isn't he?"

"No, he isn't. He's a flycop who keeps sticking his nose in places where it doesn't belong. What are you really doing here, Quincannon?"

"I'm not at liberty to say without permission of my client."

"And who would that be?"

"James Willard, the brewery's owner."

"Yes? Is he here now?"

"No. Away at a meeting. But he should be back soon."

Murmurs of surprise had rippled through the listening workmen. One of them piped up, "I saw this man chasing Mr. Lansing through the fermenting room a while ago."

"Is that so. Who's Lansing?"

"The assistant brewmaster," Malloy said. "The man who shot himself."

"Shot himself, eh? You're sure this flycop didn't do it?" His tone implied that he'd like nothing better.

Quincannon said, "I had no reason to, nor could have done it if I had. I have no key to these doors—both of which were locked by Lansing when I got here. And still are, as you'll soon see."

"Then why were you chasing Lansing?"

"I can't say without permission of Mr. Willard."

Elias Corby stepped forward. "It couldn't have anything to do with Otto Ackermann's death, could it? That was a tragic accident."

"What's that?" Kleinhoffer said. "There's been another death here recently?"

"Last week. Poor Otto, our brewmaster, slipped off a catwalk and drowned in a vat of fermenting beer. A terrible way to die, terrible. But it was an accident, as I said. The precinct officers who came to investigate ruled it as such."

"First the brewmaster, then the assistant brewmaster—an accident and an apparent suicide. Sounds fishy to me. Well, Quincannon? Is there some sort of connection or isn't there?"

"I can't say without—"

Kleinhoffer snapped, *"Scheisse,"* glared daggers at him, and then turned to Malloy. "You have the key? All right, open the doors and let's have a look at the stiff."

Malloy hastened to do his bidding. Kleinhoffer and his usual shadow, a burly sergeant named Mahoney, shouldered their way inside, taking the foreman with them. Quincannon made no attempt to join them; it was unnecessary—he'd already seen all there was to see in the utility room—and Kleinhoffer wouldn't have allowed it anyway. The other coppers, four bluecoats, held him and the rest of the onlookers at a distance.

The Prussian and his shadow blundered around inside for ten minutes, making a good deal of noise in the process. The workmen all gave Quincannon a wide berth, as if he'd been revealed as a none-too-savory and possibly dangerous spy. When the two plainclothesmen reappeared, Kleinhoffer attempted to question Quincannon again, using thinly veiled threats this time. This tactic got him nowhere, the threats being nothing but empty bluster. Grumbling, he and Mahoney proceeded to interrogate Jack Malloy and several other employees, none of whom had anything pertinent to tell.

Two nearly simultaneous arrivals put a halt to the questioning. First came the morgue wagon and a pair of attendants with a stretcher, followed less than a minute later—and not a moment too soon, by Quincannon's reckoning—by Mr. James Willard.

"Caleb Lansing, a murderer and a thief," Willard said in mournful tones. "My God, I can hardly believe it."

"There's no doubt he was guilty of both crimes," Quincannon said.

Kleinhoffer said sourly, "So you say. How do you know he killed the brewmaster for the steam beer formula? According to the bookkeeper, the official verdict is that Ackermann drowned accidentally."

"The official ruling was wrong."

"Smart flycop. Think you know everything."

"Murder when murder's been done for profit, yes."

The three men were in Willard's office, where they'd gone for the sake of privacy. The news of Lansing's betrayal and apparent suicide—a second death by violence in the Golden State in a week's time—had shocked Willard into a lather; his florid features were mottled, veins bulged and pulsed in both temples as if he might be in danger of a seizure. After a brief consultation out of Kleinhoffer's hearing, he had agreed to permit an explanation of why he'd hired a detective to investigate Otto Ackermann's demise. Which Quincannon had then given as succinctly and in as little detail as possible. It was not yet time to hand over the burned note fragment he'd found, or to reveal the presence of the two thousand dollars in the strongbox hidden in Lansing's rooms—the latter in particular, given Kleinhoffer's less than stellar reputation for honesty.

"All right, then," Kleinhoffer said when he'd finished. "How'd you get onto Lansing?"

"Astute detective work, naturally." Quincannon resisted adding that such was something the beefy dick knew little about.

"That doesn't answer my question."

"Under the circumstances the exact nature of my investigation is my and my client's concern, not the police's."

"The stolen formula is police business."

"Only if my client chooses to make it so."

"Well? Do you, Mr. Willard?"

"No."

Kleinhoffer ground his yellowed teeth. "What did Lansing do with the formula?" he demanded of the brewery owner. "Who hired *him*?"

Willard glanced at Quincannon, who imperceptibly shook his head. "I don't know."

"Meaning you're gonna be as closemouthed as the flycop here."

"Meaning I don't know. Neither does Mr. Quincannon, or he would have said so."

"Lansing may not have been hired by anyone," Quincannon said glibly. "He may have acted with the idea of selling the formula to the highest bidder. I'll find out, in any case, if Mr. Willard should want me to continue in his employ."

"I do," Willard said.

Kleinhoffer said, *"Scheisse."*

Quincannon suppressed a grin. "Are you satisfied that Lansing's death was a suicide?" he asked.

"Couldn't be anything else," the Prussian admitted grudgingly. "You trapped him down there in that utility room and he took the coward's way out."

"So he must have been guilty as I've charged."

"Or just plain off his trolley."

"In any event, as far as the law is concerned the case is

closed. There's no need for you to concern yourself with the stolen formula, Lansing's motives, or anything else to do with the matter."

Kleinhoffer repeated his favorite word. But he had no choice then except to remove himself, which he proceeded to do after jabbing a rigid forefinger in Quincannon's direction and saying ominously, "Our paths are bound to cross again, flycop. And when they do, you might well find yourself on the blunt end of my nightstick."

Empty threats bothered Quincannon not a whit. "I wouldn't count on it," he said.

When the dick had slammed out, Willard released a heavy sigh and sank into the creaking swivel chair at his desk. Through the window behind him, fog lay over China Basin and the bay beyond; tall ships' masts were faintly visible through its drift, like the fingers of skeletal apparitions. Quincannon remained standing, packed and lit his pipe, and puffed furiously to create an equivalent fog of tobacco smoke. The good rich aroma of navy plug helped mask some of Golden State's insidious pungency.

The brewery owner said at length, gloomily, "I don't suppose there's any chance Lansing hadn't yet turned the recipe over to West Star?"

"Little, I'm afraid. Assuming, that is, Ackermann relinquished his master copy before he died."

Willard brightened a bit. "You think he might not have?"

"It's possible."

"But the safe in his office where he kept it was empty . . ."

"He may have transferred the formula elsewhere for some reason."

"Yes, but . . . would Lansing have pitched him into the fermenting vat if he hadn't gotten the recipe?"

"The act could have been unintentional, the result of a struggle on the catwalk. Lansing wasn't the sort to have jumped into the vat himself to save Ackermann from drowning, no matter what the impetus."

"What are the chances it did happen that way? Be honest now. Do you believe it's likely?"

The answer to that was no, and it would not have been proper to continue giving Willard what amounted to false hopes. Ackermann's office safe had been unlocked as well as empty, and his rooms on Clay Street, which Quincannon had examined, had not been searched. The probable scenario was that the brewmaster had been forced to open the safe and then, once the formula had been pilfered, taken to the catwalk and cast into the vat. The charred note and the two thousand dollars in Lansing's flat also testified to the likelihood that West Star was now in possession of the recipe.

Quincannon believed in being straightforward with a client—up to a point. He said, "No, sir, I don't," and proceeded to explain his reasons. All, that is, except for his conviction that Caleb Lansing had been murdered; he was still not ready to confide his suspicions in that regard. He also showed Willard the burned paper with its *X.J.* signature.

"By God, this proves Lansing was in cahoots with West Star."

"To our satisfaction, yes. But not from a legal standpoint."

"You can testify as to where you found it."

"Yes, but as you can see, Lansing's name appears nowhere

on what's left of the note, nor is the remainder of its contents legally incriminating."

"But the two thousand dollars . . ."

"He could have gotten it any number of ways. Gambling, for one. There is no clear-cut connection between the money and Xavier Jones or Cyrus Drinkwater."

Willard made a faint sound in his throat that might have been a moan. He put his face in his hands and said through splayed fingers, "So there's nothing I can do. If West Star does have the recipe, there are no grounds for an injunction to prevent them from implementing it."

"You still have the copy that he gave you."

"Yes, in my safe-deposit box. But that was two months ago. He was always making refinements—he may have made more since then. Even if he didn't . . . the competition, man, the competition." Willard made the moaning sound again. "That damned Drinkwater. What I wouldn't give to see the scalawag behind bars."

"That may yet be possible," Quincannon said.

"What do you mean?"

"Your hands are legally tied, Mr. Willard, but mine aren't. I may be able to prevent West Star from implementing your formula."

Willard lowered his hands, raised his head. "How?"

"By proving that Drinkwater and Jones are behind the theft."

"Can you do that?"

"If humanly possible, I can and will." Quincannon's pipe had gone out; he paused to relight it. "Do you have a key to the cellar storeroom doors?"

"Why do you ask that?"

"I'll need one to examine the area in private once the police have gone."

"But why? Lansing's suicide has nothing to do with West Star possessing Otto's formula."

Ah, but it does. More than just a little, I'll wager. But he said only, "It pays to be thorough, Mr. Willard. No stone left un-turned. *Do* you have a key I can borrow?"

Willard had one, a master key. Quincannon departed with it tucked inside his vest pocket.

6

SABINA

Her first stop was the Montgomery Street offices of Stennett, Tyler, and Dubois, attorneys-at-law. Harold Stennett was in court, she was told, but she was granted an audience with another of the partners, Philip Dubois. Yes, he knew of the Chicago firm of Hazelton and Bean, and confirmed that Mr. Stennett had recently visited that city and had had occasion to consult with Mr. Hazelton, whom he knew from previous dealings. Dubois provided the firm's address, but no other pertinent information. He knew nothing of Charles Percival Fairchild II or matters regarding his estate, nor of an attorney named Roland W. Fairchild.

Sabina was almost but not quite satisfied. It wasn't that she doubted Roland Fairchild's story, but her years with Stephen and the Pinkertons and her time with John had taught her to accept no one and nothing at face value and to always be as thorough as possible. So she walked back to Market Street and the telegraph office near the agency, where she composed a wire to Leland Hazelton at Hazelton and Bean, Chicago, requesting verification that Roland W. Fairchild had been empowered to engage Carpenter and Quincannon, Professional Detective Services, to locate Charles Percival Fairchild III.

She debated whether or not to wait for a reply before beginning the hunt. No need, she decided. The direct starting point she'd decided upon earlier was something of a long shot, and in any case committed her to no other action just yet.

Dr. Caleb Axminster was one of the city's more successful physicians, his practice catering almost exclusively to the upper strata of society. Sabina had never been to his medical offices on Sutter Street, but she expected them to be large and rather elaborate and so they were. The reception room was not quite as sumptuously furnished as the Axminster mansion atop Russian Hill, but nonetheless tastefully appointed; his office would be likewise, she was sure, and his examining room and surgery were certain to contain only the most up-to-date equipment.

A white-uniformed nurse and an expensively dressed matron occupied the reception room. Sabina handed the nurse one of her cards and requested a brief audience with Dr. Axminster on a private matter. She was a personal acquaintance of the doctor's, she said, stretching the truth only a little, and promised to take up no more than five minutes of his time. The nurse seemed dubious, the more so after she'd examined the card, but she had been trained to be deferential; she agreed to do as asked when the doctor finished with his current patient.

Sabina sat down to wait. The matron, heavily corseted, her obviously dyed hair partially covered by a rather silly, flower-decorated bonnet, glared at her and grumbled irritably, "The nerve of some people. Why couldn't you have made a proper appointment as I did?"

"A business matter, madam. My apologies, but surely you won't mind waiting an extra five minutes."

"Surely I do mind. Do you know who I am?"

"No. Do you know who *I* am?"

"No, and I don't care."

Sabina smiled sweetly. "My sentiments exactly."

The woman muttered something rude under her breath, which Sabina ignored. She focused her thoughts on Dr. Axminster and the man he still considered, so far as she knew, to be the genuine Sherlock Holmes.

It was at the doctor's mansion that John had first encountered the bogus Sherlock, during his investigation into the series of home burglaries that had developed into the Bughouse Affair. The man she now knew to be Charles Percival Fairchild III had been Dr. Axminster's houseguest at that time, courtesy of a mutual acquaintance in the south of France; he had beguiled the physician and his wife and small coterie of friends into believing his outlandish claim that after miraculously surviving his battle with archenemy Professor Moriarty at Reichenbach Falls, he'd decided to remain "deceased" instead of returning to his practice in London and eventually made his way to San Francisco on some sort of secret mission. He had stayed with the Axminsters throughout his involvement in the Bughouse Affair and for a short period afterward. He may or may not have had recent contact with the doctor; anything was possible where "that conceited crackbrained popinjay," one of John's more colorful descriptions, was concerned.

Her wait was relatively short. A second uniformed nurse

appeared, apparently to summon the still glowering matron, and it was she who took in Sabina's card instead. She reappeared after only a minute or so, and announced that Dr. Axminster would see her immediately.

His office was also handsomely appointed, with a row of windows overlooking the busy thoroughfare below. Dr. Axminster stood before a rosewood desk waxed to a high gloss, a short, round-faced man with a Lincolnesque beard and ears that John had described to her as resembling the handles on a pickle jar.

"My dear Mrs. Carpenter," he said, smiling and taking her hand, "this is an unexpected pleasure. It has been some time since we last met. More than a year, isn't it?"

"Yes, in the offices of Great Western Insurance. I hope you'll forgive me for breaking into your busy schedule this way, Doctor, but I really won't keep you more than five minutes."

"Not at all, my dear lady, not at all." Axminster was addicted to horehound drops, a paper sack of which sat on the desktop; he popped one into his mouth. "What may I do for you? You haven't a medical complaint, I hope?"

"No, nothing like that. It concerns Mr. Sherlock Holmes. I'm trying to locate him for a rather important reason."

"Ah, I see. Quite a character, Mr. Holmes. That iconoclast Ambrose Bierce called him an imposter in one of his *Argonaut* columns, likened him to the infamous Emperor Norton if memory serves—a spurious claim if ever there was one. He's not only the genuine Holmes but every bit the brilliant detective he is reputed to be. Not," Axminster added hastily, "that you and Mr. Quincannon aren't his equal."

"Thank you. Have you had any contact with him recently?"

"No, I'm sorry to say. Not since he left my home shortly after the events last year. Left rather abruptly, as a matter of fact, without so much as a by-your-leave. Ah, well, that's genius for you, eh?"

Lunacy, too. Not that the two are so far apart.

"Do you have any idea where I might find him?"

"I'm afraid not. My wife and I were of the opinion that he'd left the city and returned to England."

"He was still here in October," Sabina said. "He popped up briefly during a case I was investigating at the time."

"Indeed? Well, well. I wish I'd known—I would have invited him to partake of our hospitality again. I really did enjoy having a gentleman of his obvious breeding under my roof. Amusing fellow, possesses all sorts of esoteric knowledge. Quite an accomplished violinist, as well."

Sabina remembered the strange, not very harmonious melody the man had been playing when she and John had visited him at the Axminster home. Accomplished violinist? As John would say, "Bah!"

Axminster sucked with obvious pleasure on his horehound drop. "You have reason to believe Mr. Holmes is still somewhere in the city, Mrs. Carpenter?"

"No. Merely the hope that he is."

"Need his assistance on another case, eh?"

"Let's just say it's a professional matter."

"Oh, of course, not at liberty to discuss it. I understand perfectly. Well, I do hope Mr. Holmes is still among is. If so, and you locate him, give him my regards and ask him to come calling again."

"I'll do that," Sabina lied. She thanked the doctor for his time and took her leave.

An answering wire from Leland Hazelton in Chicago was waiting upon her return to the telegraph office. Roland W. Fairchild was indeed authorized to act on the firm's behalf in the search for Charles Percival Fairchild III. Time was of the essence—kindly proceed with all dispatch.

Yes. She would do just that.

Carpenter and Quincannon, Professional Detective Services, made use of several reliable informants. The two Sabina depended on most often were the "blind" newspaper vendor known as Slewfoot, and Madame Louella, a fortune-teller who claimed to be a native of a Transylvanian tribe of Gypsies but who had in fact made her way west from Ashtabula, Ohio. Both had developed strings of contacts in the Barbary Coast, the Uptown Tenderloin, the waterfront areas, and the various working-class neighborhoods.

Madame Louella had been of considerable help during the Body Snatchers Affair the previous fall, so Sabina went first to her Kearney Street parlor. The woman sat alone in her "fortune room" like a spider waiting to ensnare a fly, her large body draped as usual in a flowing gold robe emblazoned with black and crimson cabalistic signs, her head covered by a somewhat moth-eaten gold turban. She had heard of the bogus Sherlock, though not in recent memory. Her vow to have him found in short order, followed by a wheedling request for a few dollars in advance—"I'm in arrears on my rent, dearie, and living hand to mouth"—were as familiar as her outfit. Madame Louella was a competent snitch, but no miracle worker, and a chronic poormouth. Sabina left her with nothing more than the promise of a successful finder's fee of twenty dollars.

Slewfoot occupied his usual stand on the corner of Market and O'Farrell. Checkered suits were his normal mode of dress; the one he wore today was an eyesore of brown and bilious yellow. He, too, knew nothing of the whereabouts of the elusive S. Holmes. Sabina made him the same offer as the one to Madame Louella, which satisfied him. He knew better than to make rash promises and to ask for cash in advance.

The likelihood of either Slewfoot or Madame Louella producing the desired results was thin at best. If Charles the Third *was* still somewhere in or near the city, he would surely be using another of his assumed names and dressing in costumes other than his distinctive Sherlockian outfit. In order for one of the informants' sources to locate him, he would have to be identified first—a difficult if not impossible task. Sabina held out little hope that this would or could be done.

The last of her tactics was the most likely to succeed, though it, too, was problematical. The shrewd addlepate might regularly peruse the city's newspapers, and then again he might not.

She went to the downtown offices of the *Morning Call,* the *Examiner,* and the *Evening Bulletin*—the last even though it was an exploitative sheet that employed the most obnoxious of muckracking reporters, Homer Keeps, with whom she and John had had run-ins in the past. At each she placed the same advertisement in the personals section, to be run immediately and for a week's duration.

> **S. Holmes please contact colleague S.C.**
> **earliest convenience. Most important.**

If he saw that cryptic little message, it ought to be more than he'd be able to resist no matter what he was up to.

7

QUINCANNON

Quincannon waited until late afternoon to conduct his search of the brewery storerooms. He left Golden State after his conference with James Willard, went to a nearby saloon to curb his always prodigious appetite with a mug of clam juice and its generous free lunch. Over a second mug, he reviewed the morning's events in an effort to piece together the puzzle.

Half an hour of this produced what he felt certain must be the why of Caleb Lansing's sudden dispatch, and a small part of the how. The rest of the how and the who continued to elude him. More information was needed in order to complete his deductions—some of which, if the gods were with him, he would discover in the storerooms. A clue, mayhap, if not actual evidence.

By the time he returned to Golden State, things had quieted down considerably. The loading dock was mostly deserted, some of the workmen having already left for the day. He appropriated a bug-eye lantern from the empty shipping office to supplement the weak electric light in the storerooms, then set off down the passage into the cellars. The only employee he encountered on the way paid him no heed.

With Willard's master key, he unlocked the storeroom door, slipped inside, and relocked it behind him. The scene of the murder first. The utility room contained nothing that Kleinhoffer and Mahoney had overlooked, or that he might have missed during his first brief inspection. None of the equipment that cluttered it had been disturbed; nor were there any other indications that a scuffle had taken place. The only signs of violence, in fact, were the marks in the bare earth where Lansing's body had lain.

Quincannon moved on to the room housing the sacked barley. The dusty smells of grain and burlap were thick enough to clog his sinuses and produce several explosive sneezes as he shined the bug-eye over the piled sacks. They were stacked close together, at a height of some five feet, and flush against the back and side walls. Nothing larger than a kitten could have hidden itself behind or among any of them.

He crossed into the other large room. The boxes of yeast and heavy sacks of malt, sugar, and hops stood in long, tightly packed rows along the side walls. No one could have hidden behind or among them, either. The floor at the far end wall was bare; a pair of hand trucks and a pile of empty fifty-pound hop sacks stamped with the name of a company in Oregon's Willamette Valley lay at the foot of the near end wall. Everything was as it had been when he'd looked in earlier.

Or was it?

No. Something seemed different now . . .

Quincannon stood for a time, scanning the room and

cudgeling his memory. What the devil was it? He poked at the boxes, the hand trucks, the empty hop sacks—futile effort, all of it. Something was altered, he felt sure of it, but whatever it was continued to elude him. He curbed his frustration with a counsel of patience. The room was now firmly fixed in his mind's eye; it would come to him eventually.

He used his handkerchief to clean smudges of yellow powder from his fingers, unlocked the outer storeroom door, and made sure the cellar corridor was empty before stepping out and reusing the key. Five minutes later he was mercifully free again of the brewery's enticing fragrance and on his way to catch a Market Street trolley.

Sabina, he was pleased to discover, was at her desk when he entered the offices of Carpenter and Quincannon, Professional Detective Services. Because he cared so much for her, he had grown sensitive to her moods; he was immediately aware that hers today was something new and not a little encouraging. She seemed more pleased than usual to see him, her welcoming smile a bit brighter and with a touch of warmth normally lacking in her professional demeanor. And was that a speculative gleam in her brown-eyed gaze, as though she might at long last be measuring him as a potential suitor?

Yes. It was neither imagination nor wishful thinking—he was certain of it. Her attitude toward him was definitely softening, as her willingness to accept his invitations to social engagements over the past few months indicated. It surely must be, then, even though she refused to say so, that she was no longer adamant that their relationship remain a business-only one.

Quincannon's pulses quickened at the thought. He beamed at her. "You look lovely today, my dear," he said, which was no exaggeration. Her shirtwaist was pale blue, with a large cameo at the throat of its high collar; her skirt was of soft gray wool which covered perfectly formed ankles (he'd had all too fleeting glimpses of them now and then); and her black hair, drawn back into its usual chignon and fastened with an ivory comb, glistened silkily in the electric light. "If I may say so."

"You may. No woman is immune to a genuine compliment."

Her response was likewise encouraging. So was the faint flush of color that tinted her cheeks. He warned himself to continue to proceed with caution—and then made the mistake of disobeying the warning by saying without weighing the words in advance, "No woman is more deserving. I've many more to pay you, though perhaps in more intimate surroundings."

Abruptly the gleam in her eyes vanished. "Is the prospect of intimacy why you're grinning like the Cheshire cat?"

Quincannon hadn't realized that he was. He abolished the grin and hid his perplexity by fluffing his whiskers. Just that quickly her demeanor had shifted from mildly (very mildly) flirtatious to coolly businesslike. Women and their mercurial moods! If ever a man were to devise a mathematical equation that satisfactorily explained them, he would be hailed as a genius greater than Archimedes or Sir Isaac Newton.

He repressed a sigh and asked how her day had gone.

"Reasonably well. Marcel Carreaux and Andrew Rayburn were here to finalize arrangements."

"Who? Oh . . . the security job for that traveling exhibit at the Rayburn Gallery. Handbags Across the Years or some such."

"Reticules Through the Ages."

"A handsome fee, as I recall, for what is bound to be a dull and uneventful undertaking. Any Barbary Coast or East Bay scruff caught snaffling handbags, even ones bristling with gems, would be the butt of jokes by his fellows for the rest of his days."

"Be that as it may, our clients consider the security necessary. And you needn't worry about having to attend."

"For which I'm grateful. Your day was much better than mine, I must say."

"Oh? Things didn't go as planned at the brewery?"

"No. I've spent the day in the company of louts and knaves, one of them a corpse."

"Corpse? Whose?"

"Caleb Lansing, the man responsible for the murder of the brewmaster and theft of his steam beer formula. One of the men, I should say. Lansing himself was murdered this morning under bizarre circumstances."

"What happened?"

Quincannon crossed to sit at his desk, where he proceeded to clean the bowl of his briar with a penknife while he gave Sabina a somewhat encapsulated account of what had taken place at the brewery. Her eyes widened as he spoke, and when he was done she said, "I don't see how Lansing's death could have been murder and not suicide. He died alone behind two locked doors, one of which you say you had under surveillance."

"Four good reasons, all of which escaped everyone's notice except mine. First, he had no weapon when I braced him in the fermenting room. A pistol the size and shape of a LeMat would have made a conspicuous bulge in his clothing. And if he had been armed, he surely would have drawn down on me instead of running like a frightened rabbit."

"He could have smuggled it into the utility room earlier and stashed it somewhere, couldn't he?"

"Planning to take his own life when he had enough money hidden in his rooms to flee the city? And to do it there in the brewery, rather than in the privacy of his rooms? No, Caleb Lansing was murdered, and for the same reason Otto Ackermann was."

"The other reasons you're so certain?"

"Second is the location of the fatal wound. Lansing was shot on the left side of the chest, just above the rib cage—an awkward, nearly impossible angle for a self-inflicted wound. Most gunshot suicides choose the head or chest as their target, for the obvious reason."

"Yes, that's true."

"Third, there were no powder burns on his shirt or vest. He was shot from a distance of at least two feet, an outright physical impossibility if his were the finger on the trigger. And fourth, he made no effort to leave the premises while leading me a merry chase, but headed straight down to the storerooms. That suggests a purpose that had nothing to do with hiding, for there was no safe place he could have concealed himself there."

"What purpose?"

"My suspicion," Quincannon said, "is that a rendezvous

had been arranged in the utility room this morning. It's seldom used, I was told. Lansing was consulting his watch when I found him in the fermenting room. That, too, is suggestive— that the time of the meeting was near at hand."

"A meeting with whom? Whoever killed him?"

"Yes. His accomplice in the theft of the steam beer recipe and the murder of Otto Ackermann."

Sabina considered this for a few seconds before she asked, "Why would Lansing need an accomplice? From what you've told me, Ackermann was an old man. It would hardly take two to coerce the combination to his safe from him and then to pitch him into the vat."

"The plan required a certain amount of brain power, daring, and strong nerve, and Lansing had none of these. The accomplice may well have been the one recruited by Cyrus Drinkwater and/or Xavier Jones. He may also have had a hold of some sort on Lansing to force him into the crime."

"You suspected all along there were two Golden State employees in cahoots, then?"

"Naturally," Quincannon lied. He *should* have suspected it from the first, given Lansing's weak-stick nature. But he hadn't until the discovery of the assistant brewmaster's corpse. Well, even the best detectives suffered a blind spot now and then. Not that he would ever admit it to Sabina, or a client or any other party.

"Was the shooting premeditated or a spur-of-the-moment crime, do you suppose?"

"A combination of both."

Sabina raised an eyebrow. "That would seem to be a paradoxical statement, John."

"Not really. When Lansing escaped from me, he fled to the storerooms to tell his partner the game was up. He was the sort who would spill everything in an instant once he was captured, and the accomplice knew it. He had no choice but to dispose of Lansing then and there, before his name was revealed to me."

"Then he was the one armed with the LeMat revolver?"

"Either that, or he planted it there himself earlier. Which means he planned to eliminate his partner for reasons of greed, self-protection, or both—his purpose in arranging the utility room meeting."

"And how did he manage after the shooting to escape from behind two locked doors and under your watchful eye?"

Quincannon fluffed his whiskers. "I can't say just yet."

"Meaning you have no idea?"

"A glimmering of one, yes." This was another prevarication. And Sabina wasn't fooled; he could tell by the look in her eye. As was his wont when he was temporarily embarrassed, he resorted to bluster. "I'll soon have the answer. No conundrum stumps John Frederick Quincannon for long, as you well know, my dear."

The corners of Sabina's mouth quirked with wry amusement. "Oh, yes, I'm well aware of your prowess. You're the rival of Vidocq and Sherlock Holmes when it comes to solving the seemingly insoluble."

"You're referring to the genuine Holmes, I trust, not that insufferable rattlepate charlatan who kept plaguing us last year."

"Well, he did help us solve several difficult crimes."

"Bah. Sheer lunatic luck in every case."

The very thought of the crackbrain Sherlock raised Quincannon's blood pressure. He finished scraping the cake from his pipe bowl with an angry swipe, scowled at the black residue on the knife blade, and produced his already soiled handkerchief to cleanse it.

Sabina, watching him, said, "What's that yellow residue?"

"Eh? Yellow?"

"On your handkerchief. Yellow and black streaks now, a fetching combination."

Quincannon peered at the saffron marks. "Oh, they came from—" He broke off abruptly, blinking, his mind filling with a memory image of the last storeroom he'd investigated.

"It's an odd color," Sabina said. "What is it?"

The answer, that was what it was. Thunderation! Why hadn't he realized it before? Excitement seized him; he bounced to his feet, stuffed pipe and closed penknife into his coat pocket, and crossed quickly to the hat rack for his derby.

"John? Where are you off to in such a hurry?"

"To the public library. And after that, if all goes well, to nab a double murderer."

8

QUINCANNON

It was well past dark when he once again arrived at Golden
State Steam Beer. The night guard at the front entrance had
evidently been briefed on the fact that Quincannon was in
James Willard's employ; a look at his credentials and he was
allowed admittance with no questions asked.

The business offices on the second floor were all deserted,
which suited Quincannon's aim perfectly. The door to the cubicle he sought was locked, but only for less than a minute
once he set to work with his picks.

He found what he'd hoped to find almost immediately—a
yellow smear on one chair leg, and two small dried flower buds
on the floor beneath the desk. Hop buds. And the yellow stuff
was lupulin, a fine powdery dust that clings to the yellow glands
between the petals of hop flowers, some of which is released
when the flowers are picked. It was this dust, not the hop buds
themselves, that offset the sweetness of malt and gave beer its
sedative and digestive qualities. A book at the public library
at Civic Center had informed him of these facts, complete
with pictures. The book had also imparted another tidbit of

information, one which made the balance of the day's events crystal clear.

Now he knew how Caleb Lansing had been murdered behind locked doors, by an assassin who had seemingly vanished into thin air.

And that assassin, Lansing's accomplice in theft and murder, was the man he'd come to suspect it would be—the man who had popped up suddenly and without explanation soon after the discovery of Lansing's body, in a section of the brewery he had no good reason to be. Elias Corby, Golden State's long-snouted bookkeeper.

There were no cabs in the vicinity of the brewery when Quincannon emerged. He had to cover the two blocks to Market Street on shanks' mare before he found one.

As he was settling inside, one of the newfangled horseless carriages that were supposedly being manufactured in large quantities in the East, though few had yet to be in use in San Francisco, passed by snorting and growling like a bull on the charge. The confounded machines were noisy polluters that frightened women, children, and horses, but he had to admit that they were capable of traveling at an astonishing rate of speed. Too bad he hadn't the use of one himself right now; it would get him to his destination twice as fast as the hansom. Speed was not of the essence, but the sooner he confronted Elias Corby and dragged a confession from the man, the sooner he would be rewarded with the balance of his fee from James Willard.

Corby resided in a boardinghouse in the Western Addition,

a fact that Quincannon had learned by a further search of the bookkeeper's office: the addresses of all of Golden State's employees were kept on file there. He hadn't uncovered anything else of interest, but that was hardly surprising; any additional incriminating evidence against Corby, if such existed, would be found in his private quarters.

No, it wouldn't, blast the luck. He was also denied the pleasure of putting the arm on Corby immediately as well. The man was not home, and when Quincannon took the opportunity to pick the lock and search the premises, as he had Lansing's that morning, there was nothing damning for him to find. Unlike Lansing, Corby evidently kept his ill-gotten gains elsewhere; there were no loose floorboards or other hiding places here. The three rooms were sparsely furnished and kept neat as a pin, but utterly lacking in personal items of any value. The only wall adornment was an illustrated calendar from a supplier of chickens and eggs in Los Alegres, an agricultural and ranching community in the North Bay. Even the clothing in the bedroom wardrobe was mostly old and threadbare.

The Spartan atmosphere explained, perhaps, why Corby had succumbed to the temptation to turn crook and slayer. His bookkeeper's salary could not have been much, and he may well have yearned for the finer things life had to offer. But if he had been paid some or all of his blood money, he'd hoarded it just as Lansing had, though much more carefully. Had it been anywhere in these rooms, Quincannon would have ferreted it out.

Across the street from the boardinghouse was a bakery and coffee bar. He claimed a table at the window overlooking the street. The night was beset with coils of fog, and the interior warmth caused the glass to mist up a bit, but he could see the boardinghouse stoop and gaslit entrance well enough. He ordered coffee and a plate of sweet rolls, and settled down for what he hoped would not be a long wait.

It was, however. Long and ultimately futile.

Quincannon sat filling and distressing his bladder with too much weakly brewed coffee until the shop closed at ten o'clock. The only individual who entered the boardinghouse was a gent far too tall and corpulent to be Elias Corby.

Where the devil was he? It was unlikely that he'd taken it on the lammas; as far as he knew, he was under no suspicion for either Ackermann's murder or Lansing's bogus suicide. It was possible he'd been paid enough for his role in the theft of the steam beer formula to head for parts unknown and the establishment of a new life. But it would have been a foolish act to disappear suddenly, with no word to anyone, thereby calling attention to himself—and Corby, unlike Lansing, was no fool. He would surely have followed the more prudent course of remaining at his job for the present.

Unless he'd been unable to. Unless something had happened to him, too—that payment for his evil deeds had not been money but hot lead or cold steel. Would Cyrus Drinkwater go so far as to order Corby's death? He might, if the bookkeeper had been witless enough to demand more money for his deeds; a scoundrel such as Drinkwater would not take kindly to threats and an attempt at blackmail. On the other hand, he was a businessman whose shady enterprises depended on payoffs; so far as anyone knew, he had never resorted to violence. Or ever would, in all probability, except as a last desperate recourse.

Quincannon debated the wisdom of lingering in the neighborhood a while longer, but there was no telling when Corby would decide to return; it might be the wee hours if he was out spending some of his ill-gotten gains. Besides which, it was a cold night and Quincannon was tired; the prospect of shivering in doorways for even a short while held no appeal. Yaffling Corby could wait until tomorrow.

Quincannon had lived in the same bachelor digs on Leavenworth Street since his arrival in the city a dozen years before, when as an agent for the Secret Service he'd been transferred to the San Francisco field office in the U.S. Mint. He'd been a hard-drinking man in those early days, and something of a hell-raiser; the large flat had been the scene of several small but raucous parties, and more than a handful of willing young wenches had shared his bed. Not that he'd been a celibate monk since taking the pledge, leaving the Service, and establishing his partnership with Sabina. On the contrary. His appetites were as lusty as ever when it came to pleasures of the flesh, or had been until the past eighteen months or so. In that period of time, only one young lady had entered the flat in the evening and not left again until morning.

Sabina was the cause of his waning interest in casual affairs, of course. All other women seemed to pale by comparison, even those whom some men—men who valued beauty above all else—might consider more attractive. It had taken him some time to admit to himself just how strong his feelings for her were. In the beginning of their relationship, seduction had been his primary goal; but as his respect and affection for her grew, lust had evolved into passion of a much more virtuous sort. He still wasn't sure it was that nebulous emotion called love. How could he be, never having been in love before? But it must be something akin to it, for he'd never felt this way about any woman before.

Since realizing and accepting this, he'd tried over and over to convince Sabina that his intentions were gentlemanly, even honorable. Her constant refusal of his attempts at social interaction led to the obvious conclusion that she simply didn't care for him in the same way he cared for her, which saddened as well as frustrated him. But then had come the subtle change in her attitude, the acceptance of invitations to dinner, plays, concerts, the softened smiles and speculative looks. He couldn't help wondering what had brought it on. Nothing he'd said or done. A simple matter of almost daily proximity building an affection that reciprocated his own? Something to do with her failed (happily failed) relationship with that society coxcomb, Carson Montgomery, last fall? Impossible to guess what went on inside a woman's mind. Not that it really mattered why she had altered her stance, only that his ardor for her might yet be requited after all . . .

These thoughts were on Quincannon's mind as he let himself into the flat. He lit the gas in the parlor and the bedroom to chase away the evening chill. Usually, these rooms were his sanctuary and he minded not at all being alone in them, but tonight they had a different effect on him, their emptiness making him feel oddly lonely. In the five years of his partnership with Sabina, she had never once set foot in here. What would she think of the place if she ever did, with its collection of Civil War artifacts inherited from his father, the shelves of books of poetry and temperance tracts he collected, the massive rolltop desk with its overflowing clutter of papers, pipes, and tobacco canisters, the marble-topped buffet and gold-framed mirror decorated with paintings of nude nymphs? Approve? Disapprove? Lord, how he yearned to find out!

He selected one of the tracts and took it to bed with him. It was one he'd read often before, not because he subscribed to the precepts of the temperance movement—he was not against alcohol per se, only his own use of it—but because it put him to sleep more quickly than any of the others. Written and printed by a flaming zealot named Ebenezer Talbot, one of the founders of the True Christian Temperance Society, it bore the title "A Bibulous Evening with Satan" and was luridly and ungrammatically inflammatory in its denunciation of the evils of drink. He was already half asleep by the time he reached the end of page 2.

9

QUINCANNON

A light rain had begun to fall during the night and it was still slicking streets and sidewalks when Quincannon once again arrived at Golden State Steam Beer shortly before ten on Friday morning. He would have preferred not to confront and arrest Elias Corby at the brewery, after yesterday's debacle, but it was a better choice than waiting until later in the day. He was bigger and stronger than the bookkeeper, and Corby was not the sort to panic as Caleb Lansing had. The coldly calculating fashion in which he had dispatched Lansing in the utility room and subsequently escaped proved that.

The issue, however, turned out to be moot.

Corby was not in his office or anywhere else on the premises.

Impatiently Quincannon waited in the bookkeeper's cubicle. He might have revealed Corby's guilt to James Willard, but his client also had yet to put in an appearance. Just as well. It better suited him and his sense of the dramatic to reserve explanations until after all the facts in a case were known to him and the felon in custody.

Ten o'clock came and went. Still no sign of Corby. Or Willard, for that matter.

By this time Quincannon had worked himself into something of a lather. Enough of this blasted inactivity. Action was what he craved, his hands on Corby's scrawny neck if the rascal gave him even the slightest bit of trouble. He quit pacing the cubicle, as he'd been doing restlessly for the past several minutes, slapped on his derby at a forward-leaning angle, and went to determine if his quarry could be found at his boardinghouse.

The answer to that was yes. He rattled his knuckles sharply on the door, once without a response, then a second time, and if that last knock had gone unanswered he was prepared to pick the lock for another quick search. But his sharp ears picked up stirrings inside—the creak of bedsprings, followed by the muted shuffle of approaching steps.

Corby's voice, hoarse and wary, called out, "Who is it?"

"John Quincannon."

". . . What do you want?"

"Open the door and I'll tell you."

"I . . . I'm not feeling well. That's why I didn't go to work this morning. A touch of the grippe . . ."

"You'll soon feel worse if you don't open the door."

There were a few seconds of silence. Then the latch lock rattled and the door opened partway, just far enough for Quincannon to see that Corby was in his nightshirt and that his eyes were bleary from more than just interrupted sleep. His beard-stubbled cheeks had a sunken, grayish tinge. A touch of the grippe? Bah. Severe hangover was more like it. The bookkeeper had, in fact, spent much of last night in the company of demon rum, either by way of celebration or in an attempt to assuage a guilty conscience.

"Well? If you're here on behalf of Mr. Willard—"

Quincannon said, "On his behalf and mine," and threw his shoulder against the door panel. Corby, driven into a backward stagger, emitted a bleat of protest as Quincannon entered and thrust the door shut behind him.

"What . . . what's the idea? You have no right to barge in here—"

"On the contrary. I have every right as a duly licensed upholder of the law to make a citizen's arrest."

Fear crawled into the little man's bloodshot eyes. "Arrest?"

"For the murders of Otto Ackermann and Caleb Lansing and the theft of Ackermann's steam beer formula."

"Those are ridiculous accusations. Lansing is the one who stole the formula and killed poor Otto. And he wasn't murdered, he died by his own hand—"

"It'll do you no good to lie or deny, laddybuck. I know the two of you were partners in the first crime, hired by Cyrus Drinkwater through his West Star brewmaster, Xavier Jones. And that it was your hand, not Lansing's, that put the bullet in his heart. I also know the clever method you employed afterward to avoid detection. The yellow hop dust, lupulin, gave you away."

Corby's face was a deathly gray color now. He avoided Quincannon's piercing gaze, swinging his head in wobbly arcs as if seeking an avenue of escape.

"You have two choices," Quincannon said. "You can come along peaceably to the Hall of Justice, or you can be carried there unconscious and trussed up hand and foot. Which will it be?"

Corby's desperation lasted until Quincannon, to emphasize his words, opened his greatcoat and then his frock coat to reveal the holstered Navy Colt. Then the wild look evaporated, the thin shoulders sagged; there was no resistance in him as he half staggered to the rumpled bed, sank down on it, and covered his face with splayed fingers.

"No, there'll be no bogus remorse, either. On with your clothes, and be quick about it."

Slowly, jerkily, Corby obeyed. Quincannon kept a sharp eye on him as he shed his nightshirt and reached for his shirt and pants. There had been no weapon in the room when he'd searched it the day before, and it was likely that the LeMat revolver had been the only one he'd possessed. Vigilance was called for nevertheless, but Corby made no false moves.

While he draped his skinny frame, Quincannon asked him how much he'd been paid for his theft of the formula and what he'd done with the money. Headshakes were his only response. Either the bookkeeper had been rendered mute by his fear, or more likely there was enough stubbornness left in him to avoid self-incrimination. Quincannon might have been able to get it out of him by threat or force, but inasmuch as he had no claim to the spoils he saw no reason to exert himself. Let the coppers attend to that chore once Corby was in their custody.

When Corby had donned his raincoat, they went downstairs and out onto the wet sidewalk, Quincannon maintaining a tight grip on the small man's arm. It was still raining, harder now and driven on a slant by a gusty wind; citizens with unfurled umbrellas hurried along, not all of them mindful of their surroundings. The hack that had brought Quincannon here was waiting at the curb, and as he and Corby crossed to it, a pedestrian with his head down and his umbrella canted forward came bustling toward them. Quincannon sidestepped, but not in time to avoid a glancing collision that turned him half around and broke his grip on Corby's arm. Before he could untangle himself from the fathead with the umbrella, his prisoner was off and running.

Quincannon shouted, "Corby! Halt, blast you, halt!" to no avail, and plunged after him.

Corby dodged past the front of the hansom, causing the harnessed horse to rear and the hack to buck forward, which in turn caused Quincannon to change direction to avoid the horse's plunging hooves; this allowed Corby to put a few more yards between them. He raced diagonally across the street and into a vacant lot.

Providence seemed to have cursed Quincannon with a continual scourge of foot chases. He'd been involved in more than one the previous year, there was yesterday's in pursuit of Lansing, and now here he was after Corby in yet another—none through any direct fault of his own. This one stoked his wrath to a white heat as he ran. Damned weather! Damned fools who didn't watch where they were going in the rain! Damned cheeky murdering thieves!

The lot was overgrown with tall grass, weeds, shrubs, a scattered few stunted trees. Chill wind stung Quincannon's face as he plowed into and through the wet vegetation, drawing his sidearm as he went. The footing was slippery, forcing both him and Corby to slow their headlong flight. Halfway across he saw the fugitive stumble, lurch, nearly fall; this allowed him to gain enough ground to cut the distance between them by half. He lengthened his stride, mowing down some sort of tall flowering bush.

A gnomish tree loomed up on the far side, its skeletal branches clicking and rattling in the wind. He started to veer around it—and his boot sole slid on the slick grass, then his toe stubbed against something unyielding, a tree root or rock, hidden there. He lost his balance and went down hard on his belly, skidding sideways to fetch up against the bole of the tree.

He clawed his way up the tree, panting, and got his feet under him. He still had hold of the Navy; a bloody wonder it hadn't gone off when he smacked the ground, with him on top of it. With his free hand he pawed wetness out of his eyes. Corby, he saw then, had managed to remain upright and therefore increased his lead to what it had been before. He had now almost reached the far end of the lot.

By the time Quincannon got to that point, Corby was dashing diagonally across the next street. Moments later he disappeared into a narrow alleyway between a butcher's shop and an emporium that sold carriage accessories. The number of pedestrians abroad made it prudent for Quincannon to holster the Navy before rushing free of the lot's confines. When he plunged recklessly ahead onto the cobblestones, he risked life and limb by cutting so close past a rumbling dray wagon that the driver had to swerve and yank on his brake. A string of profane oaths followed him onto the opposite sidewalk and into the mouth of the alley.

Sparse grass grew there; the rest of its narrow expanse was bare earthen ruts that the rain had turned into a quagmire. The muddy surface had impeded Corby's flight, slowing him enough so that Quincannon, heedless of the threat of another fall, had closed the gap between them to a few rods when the fugitive emerged into an equally muddy wagon yard.

The yard belonged to a business housed in a ramshackle wooden building, a sign above its wide double doors proclaiming it to be THOMAS VAIL AND SONS, COOPERAGE. Corby slid to a halt, looking for a way out of the yard. But it had no exit or entrance other than the alley. With his pursuer now almost within clutching distance, he stumbled to the doors which had been closed against the rain, dragged one half open, and hurled himself inside.

Quincannon slogged in after him. The interior of the cooperage was weakly lighted, inhabited by a trio of men in leather aprons working with hammers, saws, and lathes. Barrels and kegs of various sizes rose in stacks along one wall. The rest of the space was cluttered with tools, lumber, staves, forged metal rings.

Corby was over by the stacks, hopping back and forth in such a frenzy that spray came from his sodden clothing, searching frantically—and futilely—for a way out of the trap he'd blundered into. One of the coopers shouted something that Quincannon paid no attention to. He advanced implacably.

Corby looked at him with eyes the size of half-dollars, then dodged sideways in among the barrels. Quincannon lunged, caught the sleeve of his raincoat, but his fingers were too wet and stiff to maintain the grip. He took another step forward, brushing against one of the barrels in his haste—and in the next second, a shove from Corby sent the stack toppling over on him with a thunderous clatter.

Quincannon ducked, throwing up his arm to protect his head, just in time to keep the tumbling barrels from braining him. Nonetheless they knocked him flat to the sawdust-covered floor, and an edge of one fetched him a crack above his right ear. The blow was not sufficient to render him senseless, but it scrambled his thinking and weakened his struggles to free himself. Around him was more clattering noise, more shouting, but it all seemed to come from far off, muted by a painful buzzing in his ears.

The coopers dragged the barrels off him, helped him sit up. He had his wits and his hearing back by then. He blinked rapidly until his vision cleared. One of the coopers asked him if he was all right, a question he overrode with a growled one of his own. "Where is he, damn his eyes?"

"Gone," the cooper said. "Ran out before we could stop him."

Gone, and nowhere to be found by now. Quincannon said, "Hell, damn, and blast!" and followed this with a string of more flavorful oaths. After which he gathered himself and gained his feet without assistance.

Another of the coopers demanded in irate tones, "What's the meaning of all this? Look at the damage that's been done to these barrels."

"There was greater damage done than that. The blackguard I was after is a thief and twice a murderer."

"The hell you say. What are you, a nabber?"

"Detective."

"So who's going to pay for the damage? The city?"

No, Quincannon thought, James Willard by way of the expense account. He fished a pair of double eagles from his vest pocket, pressed them into the cooper's hand, and then walked away from them and out into the rain, more or less steadily.

His head ached where the barrel had struck him. And the blow had opened a small cut at the hairline; his fingers came away with a smear of blood when he touched it. Otherwise, except for a few bruises, the only wounds he'd suffered were to his dignity and his pride. Losing a prisoner he'd had twice in his grasp was a humiliation that put the taste of bile in his mouth and a fever in his blood. He'd find Corby, he vowed grimly, and when he did, by Godfrey, the son of a bitch would not get away again.

10

The opening of Reticules Through the Ages drew the anticipated large crowd to the Rayburn Gallery. If the hard rain of
earlier in the day had persisted, there might have been fewer
attendees, but it had moderated into a fine mist that promised
to give way soon to clearing skies. Most of the guests were
wealthy couples from Rincon Hill and Nob Hill, the women
bejeweled and outfitted in the latest fashion finery, the men in
silk hats and evening clothes; many would go on from here to
dine at one of the more elegant restaurants and thence to various entertainments. While the ladies examined and gushed
over the Marie Antoinette and other chatelaine bags on display,
the men in large part stood availing themselves of the liquor
and food buffets Andrew Rayburn and his staff had provided.

Sabina, dressed in her best evening gown, an embroidered
Nile-green brocade trimmed with lace, her silver mesh wrist
bag concealing her .41-caliber pearl-handled derringer, alter-
nated between wandering the room and taking up a position
near the entrance to make note of new arrivals. Electric light
from old gasoliers fitted with incandescent bulbs made the

large room bright as day and observation that much easier. She saw no one who looked the least bit suspicious.

The gallery itself was secure to her satisfaction. She'd made sure of this during the hour prior to the opening. It consisted of one very large room, a portion of which had been partitioned into small open cubicles where some of the *objets d'art* Andrew Rayburn specialized in—paintings, sculptures, and the like— were displayed. Others had been moved into the storeroom at the rear, to make sufficient room for the exhibit. The only entrance other than the main one in front was a thick storeroom door through which deliveries were made; this was bolted and chained from the inside. There were no other ways in or out. The storeroom was windowless, and the only windows in the main section were two large plate-glass ones that flanked the entrance.

Among the early-arriving guests were her cousin Callie French and husband Hugh, and a few individuals of both sexes that she'd met through Callie and occasionally socialized with. Some of the others, all eminently respectable, she knew by name and reputation. Marcel Carreaux presided over the exhibit, answering questions for the curious; Rayburn circulated among the guests, while his two clerks, Martin Holloway and George Eldredge, took turns welcoming the guests, replenishing the buffets, and manning the sales counter. None of the antique reticules was for sale, of course, but the various art objects that remained on display wore prominently placed price tags. Sabina was no expert on fine art, but based on what she did know of it, she considered Rayburn's prices exorbitant. Which was likely the reason no one was buying or even paying attention to those items.

She was passing near the exhibition again when Callie, resplendent in a blue organdy gown with extravagantly puffed sleeves, her blond hair intricately coiled as usual, approached her. "Oh, my dear, it's such a magnificent collection! The Marie Antoinette . . . why, I've never seen anything quite so breathtaking."

Her cousin had a tendency to gush when she was excited. Sabina smiled and agreed that the Marie Antoinette was a remarkable historical piece.

Callie drew her aside, into an unoccupied spot near one of the pedestal-displayed sculptures. "I really do wish you'd limit your professional activities to this type of endeavor, Sabina. It's much more befitting a lady, even a lady detective, and considerably less dangerous."

"So you've said before."

"Yes, and perhaps one day you'll heed my words."

"Perhaps."

"You certainly won't have any trouble in these genteel surroundings, I'm sure of that."

"I hope you're right."

"Of course I am. Oh . . . I see Hugh gesturing this way, I think he wants me to meet someone. We'll talk again later." Callie patted her arm and flounced away.

Sabina had known her since her childhood in Chicago, and their friendship had blossomed again after she discovered that Callie, too, had moved to San Francisco. Her cousin had married Hugh French, a protégé of her banker father, in a lavish wedding that had cost the princely sum of fifty thousand dollars, and Hugh had in turn built himself a considerable fortune in stock market speculation; they had been Sabina's entry into the sphere of the city's elite, which had led to more than one discreet job for Carpenter and Quincannon, Professional Detective Services.

But Callie constantly fretted over the hazards of detective work, and longed to see Sabina "settle down" to home, hearth, and motherhood. An inveterate matchmaker, she had been instrumental in promoting Sabina's brief liaison with Carson Montgomery. She approved of John as a potential mate, too, though warily because of his work and because of what happened to Stephen. She would be ecstatic to know that her cousin was considering even a mild dalliance with her business partner, which was why Sabina had no intention of confiding in her.

She made her way over to the food buffet. If one could call cheese, crackers, nuts, skewered pieces of fruit, and a variety of canapés food. On impulse she sampled one of the canapés. *Wrong choice. Olive and anchovy paste. Blah!*

A man whose large corporation strained the buttons of his lacy white shirt stepped past her and stood studying the offerings. This fellow has never missed a meal, she thought—words her late mother had been prone to utter in public in embarrassingly loud tones. And every one of those meals seemed to have expanded his stomach while leaving the rest of him more or less normal size. Then she chided herself for being unkind. He didn't partake of any of the food, possibly because none of it appealed to him or perhaps because he was on a diet.

He caught Sabina's eye, smiled, and chose to compliment the table. "A sumptuous buffet, is it not?"

"Very nice."

The corpulent man persisted. "Allow me to introduce

myself. Thaddeus Bakker, of the Sacramento Bakkers. Quite a prominent family, if I do say so myself. Perhaps you've heard of us?"

"Of course," she said politely, although she had not.

"May I ask your name?"

"Sabina Carpenter."

"A pleasure, Miss Carpenter. Or is it missus?"

"Missus." She didn't add that she was a widow.

"Ah. A most excellent exhibit, wouldn't you say?"

"Yes. Are you a connoisseur, Mr. Bakker?"

"Of antique handbags and reticules?" The idea seemed to amuse him. "No, no, merely an art lover and a student of history in all its forms. And you, Mrs. Carpenter? A connoisseur?"

"You might say that, yes."

The lack of encouragement in her voice for further dialogue wasn't lost on him. "If you'll excuse me, I believe I'll have another look at the exhibit." He moved away ponderously toward the display table.

One of the clerks, Martin Holloway, a small man with delicate features and taffy-colored hair, appeared with a plate of creamy cheese wedges—French Brie, evidently. He directed a brief and somewhat harried smile at Sabina before hurrying off. One of the guests, a man with a tortoiseshell pince-nez, stepped out to squint through its lens at the Brie wedges as if he found them suspect. "Harrumph!" he exclaimed three times in succession, as though something were lodged in his throat. One of the olive and anchovy canapés, perhaps, Sabina thought wryly. The portion of the one she'd eaten had not gone down well.

She started back to her observation point near the gallery entrance, only to be approached again by Callie. The velvet-cushioned settee there was unoccupied; she perched on it, not because she was tired but as a respite from the jostling crowd. The large number of bodies and the gallery's steam heat made the atmosphere close. Every time the door opened and someone entered or exited, there were welcome breaths of cold night air.

Her day had been an uneventful one. She'd heard nothing from Madame Louella or Slewfoot, nor had she had any sort of response from Charles Percival Fairchild III, alias Sherlock Holmes. Not that she'd expected or even hoped for a quick response to her personals ad; it might take days, and she might never receive any communication at all. Likely she would hear from an impatient Roland W. Fairchild again before she had any news of his elusive relative.

Andrew Rayburn appeared in front of her. Here in his gallery he seemed less fussy and more cheerful; the large turnout obviously pleased him, despite the fact that no one was buying any of the expensive art works on display. "All seems to be going quite well, Mrs. Carpenter. Quite well indeed. You've seen nothing, ah, out of the ordinary, I trust?"

"Nothing whatsoever."

"Splendid." He rubbed his hands together. "Splendid," he said again, and vanished among the guests.

Sabina stifled a yawn. Nothing out of the ordinary, nor would there be, she felt sure, the rest of this evening or either of those to follow.

The door opened and she looked up to see a tall, spare gentleman with a long mane of gray hair and a flowing beard to match, dressed in evening clothes and top hat and carrying a blackthorn walking stick. Her first impression was that he resembled photographs she'd seen of Southern military officers. But that walking stick didn't fit the image. In fact it seemed familiar—

Abruptly she stood as the newcomer turned toward her. Half hidden in the whiskers was a thin, hawklike nose and a pair of piercing eyes that regarded her alertly and with a hint of amusement. He bowed and said, "Good evening, my dear Mrs. Carpenter."

Nothing out of the ordinary? Days before I had any news of Charles the Third, if at all? How wrong I was! For there he stands, popped up like a bad penny and wearing one of his silly disguises.

"My apologies for the tardiness of my arrival," he said in his perfect imitation of a British accent. "I was unavoidably detained."

"Tardiness?"

"I trust, given the atmosphere of pleasant camaraderie in the room, there has been neither incident nor suspicious activity."

"No, there hasn't, but . . ."

He peered keenly at her. "I daresay you seem surprised to see me, dear lady. Surely you knew I would come tonight in answer to your summons."

"Summons? You mean the personals ad in the newspapers? I hoped you'd respond, yes, but . . . here, tonight?"

"Indubitably. I peruse the newspapers daily, as a private inquiry agent of stature must and as you correctly intuited I would."

"You believed the ad was a request for you to attend Reticules Through the Ages?"

"Not merely to attend the exhibition, but to offer my expertise in identifying the malefactor and preventing a bold attempt at theft. The rumors, I venture to say, are quite true."

"Malefactor? Rumors?"

"That a cunning prig after a pogue . . . excuse me, cunning thief after a prize of great value will attempt to steal the Marie Antoinette chatelaine handbag."

Sabina thought she'd banished the last remnants of her surprise and confusion, but she hadn't. Drat him, he had the infuriating knack of befuddling her—something no other man had ever been able to do. "Who? Who is going to attempt such a theft?"

"I have been unable to learn his name, or the details of his plan though it is bound to be as canny as it is bold. Have you any inklings of whom he might be?"

"No. I've not even heard those rumors you alluded to."

"You haven't? But then why did you call upon me? Surely not to assist you in routine security precautions?"

"No. I had another reason entirely."

"And that reason is?"

Before she could respond, Marcel Carreaux appeared at her side. The Frenchman hadn't heard any of their conversation, which had been conducted in low tones; his smiling, slightly flushed countenance radiated pleasure. "Ah, Madame Carpenter, all is well, eh? Ah, *bon.*" He made a sweeping Gallic gesture. "So many ladies and gentlemen have come tonight, it is most gratifying."

Charles the Third stepped forward. *"Vous devez être Mon-*

sieur *Carreaux, le conservateur de cette exposition splendide,*" he said. *"C'est un grand plaisir de vous rencontrer, monsieur."*

"Ah! *Vous parlez français! Oui, je suis Marcel Carreaux. Et vous êtes?"*

"S. Holmes, Esquire."

Sabina flinched. *Please don't tell him the S. stands for Sherlock!*

He didn't, thankfully. He said only, *"Je suis le plus heureux de faire votre connaissance aussi."*

They shook hands, beaming at each other, and continued speaking together in rapid French, with the crackbrain doing most of the talking. Sabina's command of the language was limited, but she understood enough to determine that he was saying he had been to Paris many times, "a city perhaps as grand as my native London," considered the Louvre to be the world's finest museum, and M. Carreaux blessed to have achieved the position of assistant curator.

When he finally paused for a breath, the Frenchman seized his arm and said in English, perhaps in deference to Sabina's presence, "You must come now, M'sieu Holmes, and view Reticules Through the Ages."

"And the jewel of the collection, the Marie Antoinette chatelaine handbag. Yes, I should very much like to. Will you excuse me, Mrs. Carpenter?" And off they went, arm in arm, Charles the Third saying sententiously, "If I may say so, *M'sieu le conservateur,* I have always contended that Marie Antoinette's reputation for promiscuity was exaggerated and that she was quite undeserving of the name L'Autrichienne . . ."

Sabina sat down again. She still felt bewildered, and now concerned by what Charles the Third had told her. *Was* there a plot afoot to steal the Marie Antoinette bag? His ability to ferret out bits and pieces of underworld goings-on that she and John and their various contacts knew nothing about had proven to be astonishingly accurate in the past. It was entirely possible that he'd done so again. She couldn't imagine how such a theft could be accomplished, no matter how boldly clever the thief's plan might be, with the chatelaine bag under close scrutiny at all times by herself, Marcel Carreaux, Andrew Rayburn, Rayburn's clerks, and scores of admiring and honest citizens. But she would be extra vigilant from now on. It might also be wise to try talking John into joining the surveillance. And if he wasn't willing or able, to engage one of the agency's part-time operatives for the task.

She was still considering this when the crackbrain returned a few minutes later. "Most impressive," he said. "The Marie Antoinette is exquisite, a plum ripe for the picking."

"I don't see how."

"Nor do I. But where there's a will there's a way, if I may be permitted a cliché." He sat down next to her. "Now then. You were about to tell me, when we were interrupted earlier, the reason for your personals advertisement."

Sabina hesitated. "This really isn't the proper place to discuss it. Perhaps we could meet somewhere after the exhibition closes."

"That, unfortunately, won't be possible. There is another game afoot tonight that requires my attention."

"Sometime tomorrow, then."

"Is it so important to wait until then? Why not simply tell me now?"

Again Sabina hesitated. Then she drew a breath and

plunged. "Very well. The reason for the ad is that I was hired to find you."

"Hired? By whom?"

"A Chicago attorney named Roland W. Fairchild."

His only reaction was a slight stiffening of his lean body. "I know no one of that name."

"His uncle, Charles Percival Fairchild the Second, died recently. The sole heir to the estate is his son, Charles the Third, last seen in London nearly two years ago."

He stared at her in stoic silence.

"Charles Percival Fairchild the Third," Sabina said. "That's your birth name, isn't it. Your true name."

"It is not." He spoke coldly, his eyes glittering in their nest of false whiskers. "My name is and always has been Sherlock Holmes, of 221B Baker Street, London. I answer to no other."

"Roland Fairchild and his wife are staying at the Baldwin Hotel. If you'll just speak to him—"

In one swift movement, using his blackthorn stick for leverage, he was on his feet and turning for the door.

"Wait, please—"

He didn't wait. He thrust the door open and rushed out onto Post Street. It took Sabina only a few seconds to gain the sidewalk, but by then Charles the Third had already vanished into the night.

11

SABINA

The Baldwin Hotel and Theater, on the corner of Market and Powell, was second only to the Palace among the city's luxury hostelries. Built in 1876, a year after the Palace, by a mining and real estate speculator named "Lucky" Baldwin, it was a massive structure containing nearly six hundred guest rooms and several cafés and public rooms; the accommodations in its prominent hexagonal dome five stories high were reserved strictly for ladies. The attached theater, originally known as Baldwin's Academy of Music, Sabina knew to be opulently decorated in crimson satin and gold. She had attended performances there by such touring players as Lillian Russell and Frederick Warde, and on one occasion sat in a proscenium box with Callie and Hugh to hear diminutive Della Fox sing amusing songs with such lyrics as "Just a little love, a little kiss" and "A babbling brook, a shady nook, sweet lips where kisses dwell—oh!" Hotel and theater combined took up an entire block, and though it was not as majestic as the Palace, it was grand enough to attract the rich and famous along with the simply well-to-do. The fact that Roland W. Fairchild and his wife could afford to stay there indicated both good taste and financial stability.

Somewhat reluctantly, Sabina went to the Baldwin on Saturday morning. She felt she owed her client an accounting of last evening's contact with his cousin, even though it cast her in a poor light. She'd spent a restless night, berating herself time and again over the way she had mishandled Charles the Third. She should have been more circumspect, elicited his promise to return to the gallery tonight and then tried again to arrange a private meeting. More subtle in broaching the subject of his heritage, too. She should have known he would react as he did when suddenly confronted. While he suffered from an addled self-delusion, he hadn't completely lost awareness of who he really was. He might have refused to admit it no matter where or how she braced him, but in different, quieter circumstances she'd have had a better chance of reasoning with him.

As it was, she feared that she had provoked him into fleeing the city or hiding himself so well in its darker recesses that no one could find him. In either case, she might never lay eyes on him again—a bitter prospect because it meant she'd failed in her responsibility. The one slim hope she had was his passion for the cat-and-mouse detective game, particularly a case in which he had personally involved himself. The allegedly planned attempt to steal the Marie Antoinette bag might, just might be enough to lure him back to the Rayburn Gallery, if not tonight, then on one of the subsequent evenings.

No matter what happened, she owed it to herself as well as her client to own up to her mistake and, if possible, make amends for it.

From an obsequious clerk at the desk in the Baldwin's or-
nate lobby she learned that Mr. and Mrs. Roland W. Fairchild
occupied room 311. The absence of a key in their room box
indicated that they were in residence. She waited while a bell-
hop took her card upstairs, and when he returned he conducted
her into a hydraulic elevator similar to the ones at the Palace
and left her outside the door marked 311.

Her discreet knock was immediately answered. The large-
boned woman who opened the door was approximately Sabina's age, raven-haired, attractive in a severe and rather haughty
way. No welcoming smile, merely a long appraising look out
of cool gray eyes. She wore a pinch-bodice shirtwaist that ac-
cented an overlarge bosom, and a trumpet-shaped skirt that fit
closely over broad hips and flared just above the knee. The
hourglass figure she presented, Sabina thought, was considerably aided by a tightly laced corset.

"Mrs. Fairchild?"

"I am Octavia Fairchild, yes." Her voice was as cool as
her gaze. "I must say, you're not quite what I expected, Mrs.
Carpenter."

"No? And why is that?"

"I always thought lady detectives were a middle-aged and
masculine lot. My husband didn't tell me his was young and
rather comely."

The remark was not in any way a compliment. In fact, the
reference to her being "his" lady detective was mildly insulting.

"Is Mr. Fairchild here?"

"Not at the moment, but I expect him back shortly. You may
as well come in and wait."

The sitting room was small by Baldwin standards, its windows overlooking the Powell Street cable car tracks. This coupled with the fact that it was on a lower floor and thus lacked the panoramic views of the larger rooms and suites on the upper floors, caused Sabina to revise her opinion of the Fairchilds' financial situation. Not wealthy, just moderately well-to-do. Putting up at the Baldwin, like the expensive clothing each wore, was more a façade calculated to make their station seem loftier than an expression of good taste.

Not very graciously, Octavia Fairchild invited her to sit on a tufted red plush settee. "Have you come because you've located my husband's cousin?" she asked as she lowered her corseted hips onto a matching chair.

Sabina said, "I've learned that he is still in San Francisco, yes. Or was last night."

"What does that mean, pray tell?"

"It means he responded to a personals ad I placed in the newspapers and that I spoke to him briefly."

"Why briefly?"

"Circumstances prevented a longer discussion."

"What circumstances?" Then, when Sabina didn't respond, "Did Charles consent to speak with my husband?"

"I told him he could be reached here at the Baldwin."

"That doesn't answer my question. Does he intend to speak to Roland? Does he intend to return to Chicago to claim his inheritance?"

"I don't know. I didn't have a chance to ask him."

Three horizontal lines marred the smooth surface of Octavia Fairchild's forehead. "Why not?"

"I would rather wait until your husband returns before I explain."

"That's not necessary. Roland and I have no secrets from each other."

"Just the same, I'd rather wait."

"At least tell me this," the woman said through pursed lips. "Does Charles still retain the mad notion that he is that British detective, Sherlock Holmes?"

"Yes."

"He should be put in an asylum. I've said that all along and Roland agrees with me. He's a danger to himself and quite possibly to others."

"I don't agree, Mrs. Fairchild."

"You're not qualified to judge. You hardly know the man."

"Nor do you. From what your husband told me, no one in your family has seen Charles in years."

Octavia Fairchild fixed her with a gimlet eye. Sabina met and returned the gaze stoically. This silent clash of wills lasted for some fifteen seconds; then Mrs. Fairchild got abruptly to her feet and, without a word, walked to the bedroom in an exaggerated regal stride, entered, and closed the door sharply behind her.

Sabina sat with a tight curb on her temper. She hadn't much cared for Roland W. Fairchild, and she actively disliked his wife. Among other things, the woman was artificial, overbearing, contrary, and downright rude. In short, she was what Stephen had referred to as a provider of a severe pain in the gluteus maximus.

Waiting, Sabina wondered if she might have been a little hasty in defending Charles the Third. Was he in fact a danger to others, if not to himself? She remembered the incident in

October, her discovery of the body of Artemas Sneed, the scruff who had attempted to blackmail Carson Montgomery, and her surmise that it might well have been the crackbrain Sherlock who had skewered him with a sword cane. In self-defense, if so, she'd thought at the time, but it could have been otherwise—a lunatic's premeditated act of vigilante justice. Even if she'd confronted him, Charles the Third would not have admitted to the slaying no matter what had transpired in Sneed's waterfront lair. So there was no way for her to know one way or the other.

The sound of a key turning in the door latch heralded Roland Fairchild's return. Sabina remained seated as he entered and closed the door behind him. When he spied her he halted, blinking, and glanced around the otherwise empty room. His surprise at finding her alone in the sitting room was obvious, as well it should be.

"Mrs. Carpenter," he said. "Ah . . . where is my wife?"

"In the bedroom, I believe."

"Bedroom? Why?"

Sabina had no doubt the woman was listening behind the closed door. She said, "You'll have to ask her, Mr. Fairchild."

He made a vague dismissive gesture, as if his wife's actions were of no particular consequence to him, removed his bowler hat, and seated himself in the same chair she had occupied. His attire was as natty today as it had been on Thursday, dominated this time by a Lombard houndstooth silk vest and a cravat the color of burgundy wine.

"You have news of my cousin? You've found him?"

"Not exactly. He is still in San Francisco, or was last evening, but I wasn't able to find out where he's residing."

"Then how do you know he's still here in the city? Did someone see him?"

"Yes. I did."

"Where?"

"At an art gallery on Post Street. As I told your wife, I spoke to him briefly."

"Did you tell him you know his real identity?"

"Yes."

"Well? What did he say?"

"He refused to admit it."

"Of course he still believes he's Sherlock Holmes," Fairchild said, as if he were neither surprised nor displeased at the fact. There was what Sabina took to be a hopeful note in his voice when he asked, "Is it your opinion that his delusion is such that he has completely suppressed the truth about himself?"

"For the most part, yes, though I should say he has moments of awareness."

"He may be certifiably insane nonetheless. What was his re-action to the news of his father's death and the inheritance awaiting him in Chicago?"

"None."

"To my presence in San Francisco? You did tell him I am staying here at the Baldwin Hotel?"

"Yes, but he didn't respond to that, either."

"Did you try to talk him into contacting me?"

Time to pay the piper.

"I didn't have time," Sabina said. "He fled before I could say or ask anything more."

"Fled? For what reason?"

"I'm afraid it's my fault."

A nose twitch showed Fairchild's displeasure. "Are you saying you acted inappropriately, frightened him away?"

"Somewhat rashly, yes. The circumstances were such that—"

"Hang the circumstances. Why didn't you stop him?"

"How should I have done that, Mr. Fairchild? By force?"

The bedroom door opened abruptly and out came Octavia Fairchild, dark visaged, like a cloud that robbed the room of some of its light. "A proper *male* detective would have stopped him by whatever means necessary. I told you, Roland, that hiring a woman was a foolish decision."

Fairchild aimed a narrow-eyed glance at his wife. "Eavesdropping is childish behavior, Octavia. Why didn't you simply step out here and join us? Why were you lurking in the bedroom in the first place?"

"I neither like nor approve of your Mrs. Carpenter. She was quite rude to me before you came. Rude, and quite obviously incompetent. If you ask me, she should be discharged immediately and replaced by a capable male investigator as I suggested in the first place."

"I haven't asked you. Please keep still and permit me to determine what's best."

Octavia Fairchild snapped her mouth shut and stood stiffly, arms akimbo, directing dour looks at both her husband and Sabina.

"Mrs. Carpenter," Fairchild said, "do you consider it likely my cousin will remain in San Francisco?"

"It's difficult to say for sure. For the time being, perhaps he will. He has what he considers, or rather his Sherlock Holmes persona considers, to be pressing business here."

"What sort of pressing business?"

Sabina had no intention of sharing this information with the Fairchilds. "He didn't take me into his confidence."

"Is it possible he'll contact you again of his own volition?"

"As unpredictable as I've found him to be, yes, it is. He might also decide to contact you in spite of his actions last evening, though that seems doubtful."

"And if he doesn't do either? What are your chances of locating him again?"

Unable to keep still, Octavia Fairchild said, "Slim and none, I should say. I still think you should discharge her."

"In favor of a male investigator who has had no dealings with Charles in San Francisco, doesn't know him at all?" Fairchild said this without looking at his wife.

"What about her partner, Mr. John Quincannon? Surely he is more competent than she."

Sabina said, "My partner is involved in another case that commands his full attention. Even if he were free, there is nothing he could do that I can't or haven't already."

"So you claim."

"That's enough, Octavia," Fairchild said sharply. Then to Sabina, "Well? What *are* the chances of communicating with Charles again?"

"I can't answer that. All I can tell you is that if you wish me to continue, I will do everything in my power to bring you and your cousin together." John wouldn't like what she was about to say next, but there was no need for him to know about it. She must do what she felt was right and proper. "If I fail, I will not only waive the remainder of our agreed-upon fee, but refund your retainer."

Octavia Fairchild emitted an unladylike snort. Her husband ignored her. Nose twitching again, he said, "Very well, Mrs. Carpenter. You have three days. If Charles has not contacted me in that time, with or without your assistance, I will consider our arrangement terminated, hold you to your promise regarding financial matters, and seek other options."

"Very well," Sabina said.

Fairchild showed her to the door. All the way across the room, she could feel Octavia Fairchild's hostile gaze like a dagger between her shoulder blades.

12

QUINCANNON

Elias Corby might have vanished into thin air, for all the success Quincannon had in attempting to find him after the embarrassing incident at the cooperage. He spent several hours interviewing coworkers and neighbors of Corby's, none of whom knew the man well. If the murderous crook had any close friends, male or female, or any vices such as gambling or the services of prostitutes, he'd spoken of them to no one. A closemouthed loner, from all indications.

Had he fetched his stash of money and fled the city for parts unknown? This thought gave vent to another, belated one and led Quincannon once more to Caleb Lansing's rooms. The strongbox was no longer secreted under the loose floorboard; it lay open and empty on the dining table. Damnation! Corby, of course. The none too bright Lansing must have let the location of the hiding place slip at some point in their dealings. And now the fugitive was in possession not only of his own loot but Lansing's as well—enough cash to take him a long way from San Francisco.

On the slim chance that Corby might still be holed up in the city, Quincannon put out the word among his informants and information sellers—men such as Luther James, Breezy Ned, and Ezra Bluefield. Bluefield, the former owner of a Barbary Coast deadfall called the Scarlet Lady, was a particularly reliable source of information; he owed Quincannon two debts of gratitude, one for having saved his life when a rival saloon owner attempted to puncture his hide with a bullet, the other for assisting him in his aim to become a respectable citizen by selling the deadfall and using the proceeds to purchase an Uptown Tenderloin saloon and restaurant, the Redemption, where he now held sway. But he still had his finger on the pulse of the Coast, and knew or could often find out the whereabouts of wanted lawbreakers.

No such luck in Corby's case. When no word came from Bluefield or any of his other informants by Saturday morning, Quincannon, whose patience was already worn celluloid thin, decided the time had come to take another criminal bull by the horns, wrestle him a bit, and see what could be found out from him.

Xavier Jones, for one. Cyrus Drinkwater, for another.

Jones was his first choice, so he set out mid-morning for the West Star Brewing Company. Yesterday's rain had gone and the sky was mostly clear, the February sunlight pale, the wind modulated into a cool breeze. A day made for much more pleasant activities than chasing after thieves, a fact which sharpened his determination.

West Star Brewing was situated on Jackson Street near the site of the old Adam Schuppert Brewery, California's first such enterprise established during the 1849 Gold Rush. The building was smaller than Golden State's and, according to James

Willard, produced an inferior brand of lager. But Quincannon's visit there proved to be wasted effort; Saturday, he was told, was not one of Xavier Jones's workdays.

He had obtained the brewmaster's residence, on Sacramento Street near Lafayette Park, from the city directory. But a trolley car ride there did him no good. Jones was not at home, or at least not answering his bell, and the large and well-populated building's security was such that surreptitious entry for a search of Jones's apartment would have been difficult.

Quincannon settled instead for contacting a handful of Jones's neighbors. One confided that the brewmaster's favorite idle-hour pastime was playing cribbage and that he frequented an establishment on Polk Street called the Elite Cardroom and Pool Emporium. He found his way there, only to learn that the place's elegant name was a misnomer—it was just another run-of-the-mill neighborhood gaming parlor—and that Jones was neither present nor had been there that day.

Frustration had once again begun to weigh heavily on Quincannon by this time. Thwarted no matter where he looked for Jones, as he'd been thwarted in his hunt for Elias Corby. Would Cyrus Drinkwater be easier to buttonhole? Well, he would soon find out. He'd had enough of chasing around the city on the rail lines; he hired a cab to drive him to Rincon Hill.

Drinkwater was a known habitué of the Cocktail Route, the nightly bacchanal in which wealthy businessmen of all types met with friends in one of more than twenty first-class saloons between the Reception on Sutter and Dunne Brothers at Eddy and Market, to discuss business, politics, and scandal involving others and themselves, all the while consuming copious amounts of liquor and food—a ritual that often lasted all night.

Men such as Drinkwater seldom arrived home before dawn or emerged again before noon on weekdays, usually much later on weekends.

The thought of rousing the old reprobate from his bed was a pleasing one, but he had no more luck at the lavish home than anywhere else on this day's blasted runaround. The uniformed maid who answered the door informed him that Mr. Drinkwater was not in residence. Nor did she know, or refused to tell if she did, where he could be found.

Drinkwater maintained an office in a building on Turk Street near the Civic Center. He wasn't there, either. Canvassing the array of saloons and restaurants where he might have gone to cure a hangover or fill his belly was an undertaking that held no appeal for Quincannon. He decided instead to direct his hired cab to the headquarters of the Gray Brothers Quarry Company on Sansome at Green. Drinkwater was known to make periodic rounds of his various enterprises, and his not-so-silent partnership in the Grays' operations was second only to his ownership of West Star Brewing as a major source of income.

The quarry site was the largest in the city. George and Harry Gray, that pair of equally conscienceless rogues, had been in the quarrying business for nearly thirty years. They had established their Telegraph Hill quarry and rock crusher some four years before, an ideal location for their purposes; the unstable cliff was composed of the sandstone geologists called greywacke mixed with laminated shale, a hard serpentine perfect for their manufacture of the artificial stone used for paving city sidewalks and curbs. They had blown up huge chunks of the rock face, reputedly using ninety kegs of dynamite in the original detonation—heedless of the homes perched on the hilltop nearby and the citizens who lived in them. In January of '94, one explosion caused a rockslide that crushed a duplex on Vallejo Street, but despite the fact that the owner received a $3,000 judgment against the Grays, it did nothing to bring about so much as a temporary stoppage of the careless dynamiting. It wasn't until a shoemaker's house at the corner of Union Street and Calhoun Terrace was blown off its foundation the following year that a judge issued a permanent injunction forbidding any more blasting.

But such injunctions meant nothing to such men as the Grays and Cyrus Drinkwater. The brothers opened another quarry on Douglass Street in Noe Valley, meanwhile making use of their powerful political connections and bribes to various city officials to keep that equally dangerous and damaging enterprise going. And to eventually resume their systematic destruction of Telegraph Hill in spite of the judge's "permanent" injunction.

From the look of the ruptured yellow-brown face of the hill now, the Grays' publicly stated intention to level it entirely and to then open a brick factory on the site seemed a bleak likelihood. Tons of rock already had been crushed and transported to construction sites by teams of men and horse- and mule-drawn wagons, and even though it was Saturday, what appeared to be a full crew was at work in the quarry when Quincannon arrived. The chilly, now sunless afternoon was filled with the ring of singlejack hammers breaking rock, the thunderous grinding clatter of chunks being loaded into and pulverized by the crusher, the rattle of heavily laden dray wagons departing and empty ones arriving, the profane voices of the laborers.

The quarry noise was matched by the passing clatter and rumble of railcars on the city's unique minirailroad, the Belt Line, that ran along the northeastern waterfront, servicing businesses and transporting offloaded freight from ships anchored at the busy piers. The line had begun operations in 1890 and ran for 3.2 miles from the foot of Lombard Street to the Ferry House; rail traffic south of that point was controlled by Southern Pacific. Its small roundhouse was located nearby, at the corner of Sansome and the Embarcadero. If blasting were being done at the quarry today, which at present it wasn't, the din in the area would have been deafening.

The Gray Brothers offices were housed in a plain board-and-batten building farther up Sansome, at a safe distance from the ravaged hillside. Two conveyances were parked in the wagon yard alongside, one a large four-wheeled, four-passenger, two-horse Whitechapel carriage, its liveried driver lounging on the high seat. The carriage was painted a dark maroon color with matching dusters and folding hood, the moldings decorated with a wide cream-colored stripe. It was deliberately distinctive among such equipage, often sighted on the city streets; as soon as Quincannon saw it and the waiting driver, a hulking individual named Bruno who doubled as Cyrus Drinkwater's bodyguard, he knew he'd finally found the elusive businessman.

A tired and grumpy-looking clerk—the Gray brothers, in addition to their other shortcomings, demanded long hours from their employees and paid low wages—informed Quincannon that Mr. Drinkwater had been in conference with Mr. Harry Gray for the past half hour. How long the conference would last he didn't know. Quincannon said he would wait.

His patience had worn thin and his mood was dark when the two conspirators finally emerged from the rear of the building. He had never had the unpleasure of meeting either, but their photographs had often appeared in the newspapers. They were completely different in size and appearance: Harry Gray, a large, graying, clean-shaven man with a substantial corporation over which he wore an immense gold watch chain; and Drinkwater, an inch above six feet, almost cadaverously thin, his bony face adorned with reddish Dundreary whiskers— the flowing sideburns, nearly a foot long in his case, named after those worn by the lead character in the popular British play *Our American Cousin*. Evidently their conference had been a successful one, no doubt involving money, rascality, or both; they continued to share a chuckle as they shook hands and said their good-byes.

Gray went back inside his office and Drinkwater turned toward the door. He carried a maroon-colored umbrella so tightly furled that it also served him as a walking stick. As he passed the desk, the overworked clerk said deferentially, "The gentleman there is waiting to see you, Mr. Drinkwater. He wouldn't give his name, sir."

Drinkwater's pale eyes widened slightly when his gaze rested on Quincannon, who had risen. Then he donned a falsely sunny smile. "I know his name," he said, advancing. "Though we've never had the pleasure of making each other's acquaintance. How do you do, Mr. Quincannon?"

"Well enough, considering." He accepted Drinkwater's extended hand, found it dry and leathery, and released it.

"Good, good. How did you know I was here, may I ask?"

"I didn't. I came on the chance."

"Ah. Well, sir. What is it you want of me?"

"A few minutes of your time. Private conversation on a matter of mutual interest."

The sunny smile dipped a little, sardonically. "At your service. Shall we go outside?"

They went outside and over into the side yard. The quarry sounds, dominated by the thudding grind of the rock crusher, made Drinkwater raise his voice when he said, "Rather noisy here. Tell me, do you have equipage or did you come by public transportation?"

"Hansom."

"Ah. Will you accept a ride to wherever your next destination might be? We can speak freely in the comfort of my carriage."

Quincannon saw no reason to refuse. "I will."

The Whitechapel's seat cushions were covered in tufted velvet of the same dark maroon as its exterior, and cloud soft compared to those in the hansom cabs. Quincannon had to admit that the carriage was a pleasure to sit in. And to ride in; extra strong springs kept the jarring and swaying as the wheels clattered over cobblestones to a minimum.

Once they were under way, Drinkwater asked him where he was bound and he said Market at Second Street would do. His growlingly empty stomach dictated the destination; Hoolihan's Saloon, his favorite haunt since his Secret Service days, was on Second and its free lunch second to none in his estimation.

"Now then," Drinkwater said. "What is it you wish to discuss with me, Mr. Quincannon?"

"Elias Corby, to begin with."

"Corby? I don't believe I know the man."

"And Caleb Lansing."

Drinkwater pretended to consider the name. "Lansing, Lansing. Isn't he the poor soul who committed suicide at the Golden State brewery? I seem to recall reading about that in yesterday newspapers."

"He didn't commit suicide, he was murdered."

"Murdered, you say? By whom?"

"His partner in the killing of Golden State's brewmaster, Otto Ackermann, and the theft of Ackermann's steam beer formula. Elias Corby."

"How do you know all this?"

"I'm an expert detective, as you're well aware."

"Yes, I've heard of you and your accomplishments. But this man Corby. Just who is he and why come to me about him?"

"He is or was Golden State's bookkeeper, a fact of which I believe you're also well aware."

"But I'm not. I told you, I've never heard of the man."

"Xavier Jones had dealings with him. Lansing, too."

"Jones? You mean my brewmaster at West Star? Are you suggesting he was involved in what happened at Golden State?"

"Directly involved. He's the one who hired Corby and Lansing to steal the formula."

The carriage slowed for a turn onto Market Street. Drinkwater tugged at one of his long Dundreary sideburns, sat frowning out the window for a few seconds before shifting his gaze, narrow-eyed now, back to Quincannon. "Hogwash. Why, Xavier Jones is a solid citizen, above reproach. He would never collude in such a crime."

"He would if he was ordered to."

"Who would issue such an order?"

"His employer, of course."

Drinkwater stiffened perceptibly. The muscles in his bony face worked up an expression of indignation that was patently false. He said, making an obvious effort to retain his composure, "Are you accusing me of wanton theft and suborning murder?"

"Theft, if nothing else."

"That is an outrageous falsehood. Outrageous, I say."

"James Willard doesn't think so. Neither do I."

"I don't care what Willard believes. Or what you believe, Quincannon. If you dare to make such a ridiculous accusation to the authorities or anywhere in public, I will have my lawyers sue you for slander, defamation, and grievous mental anguish."

"I won't. Not until I can prove it."

"You'll never prove it. Never."

"Won't I? I wouldn't wager against it if I were you."

Drinkwater glared at him for several seconds, his eyes glinting with the sharpness of knife points. Abruptly, then, he reached up to slide open the roof panel that allowed him to communicate with the driver. "Bruno, stop the carriage immediately. Immediately, I say!"

Bruno obeyed. The Whitechapel swerved to the curbing, came to a jolting halt. Drinkwater then pointed the ferruled tip of his umbrella at Quincannon as he would have pointed a pistol or long gun. "Get out," he said angrily. "I'll have no more of your company."

"With pleasure, sir. My thanks for the ride and the illuminating conversation."

"Get out!"

Quincannon took his time stepping down. With the door still open, he grinned in at the cadaverous rogue. "You'll be hearing from me again."

"If I do, you'll hear from my lawyers."

Drinkwater reached over to yank the door closed, then shouted up to Bruno to proceed. The carriage clattered off into the Market Street traffic.

Quincannon stood on the sidewalk looking after it, feeling well pleased with himself. He'd stirred the pot for fair and with the desired results. Satisfied himself beyond the slightest doubt that Cyrus Drinkwater was behind the theft of Otto Ackermann's steam beer recipe. And served notice that he was not about to get away unscathed.

13

SABINA

Saturday evening's attendance at Reticules Through the Ages was somewhat smaller than Friday's, despite the better weather. Still the ebb and flow of well-dressed ladies and gentlemen was substantial enough to please both Marcel Carreaux and Andrew Rayburn. Sabina, dressed in her second-best gown, a silk taffeta of pale gold, saw several familiar faces, including a few who had been present at the exhibit's gala opening. The corpulent art connoisseur from Sacramento, Thaddeus Bakker, was one; the man with the pince-nez who had seemed offended by the French Brie was another.

The one person she didn't see was Charles the Third.

She'd heard nothing from or about him after her unsatisfactory meeting with Roland Fairchild and his bitch (yes, bitch) of a wife. The small hope that he might attempt to contact her at the agency, or that word of him might come from one of her informers, had kept her there all afternoon. That hope was even smaller tonight.

But her main concern now that she was at the gallery again was the allegedly planned theft of the Marie Antoinette handbag. Was Charles the Third's suspicion valid or not? There seemed to be no way a thief, no matter how cleverly professional, could manage to steal the bag in front of the watchful eyes of herself, Carreaux, Rayburn, his two clerks, and dozens of guests. The reticules were prominently arranged on tables set behind standards of red velvet rope, the display tables well lighted; no one could get close enough to them to snatch the Marie Antoinette and hope to get away with it. To even step over the ropes, much less touch any of the bags, was forbidden and cause for immediate expulsion.

Still, no matter how addlepated Charles the Third might be, the information he had gathered and imparted in the past invariably proved to be factual. And so she was extra vigilant tonight, carefully scrutinizing each new arrival, continually circulating among the guests with one eye always on the exhibition.

"Ah, Mrs. Carpenter. A pleasure to see you again."

She turned to find Thaddeus Bakker at her elbow. His bow was rather clumsy, a product of his bulging midsection. "Good evening, Mr. Bakker. Back for another view of the treasures?"

"Indeed. San Francisco has many attractions for the visitor, but a marvelous exhibit such as this comes along but once in a lifetime. I felt I must see it at least one more time. It drew you again for the same reason, I trust?"

"Yes."

He patted his corporation. "I must admit," he said with a chuckle, "I also find the buffets to be splendid as well. A superb selection of food and drink, wouldn't you say?"

"Oh, absolutely," Sabina lied, remembering the dreadful anchovy and olive canapé she'd tasted the previous evening.

"I believe I'll partake now. Will you join me?"

"Thank you, no. I've already eaten."

Bakker bowed again and moved away to the food buffet. No sooner had he done so than Andrew Rayburn approached her. He gestured toward the fat man, who was circling the buffet with an empty plate, taking his time about making a selection from the trays. "Who is that man you were talking to?" he asked. "He was at the opening and now he's back again. You seem to know him, but I don't."

"Only since last evening. His name is Thaddeus Bakker. Of the Sacramento Bakkers. An art connoisseur."

"Ah. Well, that's all right then." Rayburn smoothed his shoelace mustache. Then he frowned twitchily and gestured again. "I don't know that fellow, either—the one in front of the display. He seems to be taking an inordinate interest in the Marie Antoinette centerpiece."

Sabina looked. It was the slight man with the pince-nez. "Just admiring it, apparently, like everyone else."

"He was at the opening as well. Do you know him?"

"No. But there is nothing suspicious about him. Another connoisseur, most likely."

"I believe I'll introduce myself. To Thaddeus Bakker as well. I am always interested in making the acquaintance of connoisseurs."

Especially those who might be in the market for the overpriced art works you sell, Mr. Rayburn.

The evening progressed. Guests came and went, ate and drank, engaged in animated conversations, and admired the antique reticules. Sabina's feet and lower back began to ache from the constant moving about; she would have liked to rest for a time on the velvet settee by the entrance, but Charles the Third's dire warning kept her from doing so. She tried to maintain a central location where she could keep watch on both the display and the entrance, but that wasn't always possible because of the shifting of the crowd.

She passed near the exhibit, where Andrew Rayburn was now standing, when a rather overdressed middle-aged dowager with great sausage-shaped curls hurried up to the gallery owner. The woman said in irritated tones, "Mr. Rayburn, I must protest. This is a refined gathering, after all."

"Protest, Mrs. Delahunt? For what reason?"

"That a suspicious individual who quite obviously does not belong among ladies and gentlemen of culture and breeding has been allowed to enter the premises and piggishly stuff himself at the buffet."

Sabina glanced toward the food buffet, but the clutch of guests nearby obscured her view. She stepped forward. "Did you say suspicious, madam?"

"I did." Mrs. Delahunt peered at her through her lorgnette. "Who are you, young woman?"

"One of my, ah, employees," Rayburn said.

"Indeed. Well, I suggest you have this . . . person removed immediately. Lord knows what he might be up to besides decimating the hors d'oeuvres. He reminds me of those dreadful Australian hooligans, the Sydney Ducks, that infested the city when I was a girl."

Sabina made her way through the knot of guests until she could see the food buffet and the man standing there filling a plate with a variety of canapés. Martin Holloway, Rayburn's clerk, was speaking to him in a low voice. A few of the remaining guests stood peering at the newcomer askance, murmuring among themselves.

Sabina had been away from the door when the man slipped inside; she hadn't seen him until now. He was dressed in a rolled-brim derby, a long-tailed broadcloth coat with red velvet collars, and baggy trousers; his hair was long, shaggy, and of an unnatural inky black color, and he wore snaky black mustaches of the sort that villains twirled in stage melodramas. A smudge of what appeared to be lampblack stained one unshaven cheek.

Her heart gave a small leap. No one in his right mind would come to an exhibit in a high-toned art gallery looking as he did, in such an atrocious disguise. No one except the one person she knew who was *not* in his right mind.

Charles the Third had returned after all.

Holloway said, "Oh, Mrs. Carpenter. This . . . person claims you know him and that he has a right to be here."

"Of course she does and I do," Charles the Third said. "Good evening, dear lady. I should have come straight to you, I know, but I daresay I'm famished. I have had no opportunity to dine the entire day."

Rayburn had joined them, looking fussily nonplussed. The crackbrain's disguise was effective enough so that the gallery owner didn't recognize him as the same man who had attended the opening in a much less ridiculous outfit. "*Do* you know him?" he asked Sabina.

"I do." *Unfortunately.*

"I am Mrs. Carpenter's assistant, as it happens."

"Assistant? But . . ." Rayburn appealed to Sabina. "But the way he's dressed . . ."

"I must apologize for that," Charles the Third said before she could speak. "I also had no opportunity to change my present costume for more appropriate attire." He smiled disarmingly at Sabina. "I must say, you have exquisite sartorial taste. Your gown this evening . . . charming, quite charming."

Sabina, caught between relief and exasperation, took hold of his arm and firmly guided him away from the buffet. On their stroll across the room he nibbled one of the canapés from his plate. "These are reasonably palatable despite an excess of mayonnaise. Wild cold-water lobster from Alaskan waters, I should say."

She could think of nothing to say. Once again, he had her at a loss for words. She steered him behind one of the low partitions, where she released his arm and shook her head to clear it.

Lord, he can be infuriating!

"I must also apologize for my tardiness," he said. "I intended to arrive promptly at six o'clock, but in the words of the commendable Scotsman Bobbie Burns, the best laid plans o' mice and men gang aft agley."

"I didn't expect you to be here at all tonight."

"And why not, pray tell?"

"Well, after our conversation last evening, and the way you dashed off . . ."

He made a dismissive gesture with his free hand. "I have decided that issue is of no consequence. Merely a matter of mistaken identity, to be cleared up at a later time."

"Cleared up how?"

"In a satisfactory manner."

"Satisfactory to whom?"

"To all concerned, naturally."

"Then you intend to meet with your cousin Roland?"

"I do not have a cousin Roland. I have a brother Mycroft, and he is my only living relative. As I will most assuredly make clear to this Roland Fairchild person."

"You still insist you're not Charles Percival Fairchild the Third?"

"Of course I do. The notion is absurd. You of all individuals in this metropolis should know that I am Sherlock Holmes, the world's foremost consulting detective."

Sabina opened her mouth, then closed it. Once more she could think of nothing to say. A cold draft led her to glance around the partition. Several of the guests had already departed and others were leaving, at least in part because of the incident with Charles the Third. The remaining visitors numbered no more than a dozen, all grouped in the middle of the room.

The crackbrain finished his last canapé, dabbed at his lips with a cocktail napkin, set the plate on a pedestal on which a bronze statuette of a nude woman rested, dusted his hands, and said, "Now then. To the matter of immediate importance to both of us. Quite obviously nothing out of the ordinary has occurred this evening."

"Only your arrival in that ridiculous disguise. Why did you claim to be my assistant?"

"I am temporarily acting in that capacity, am I not? As a result of having brought you the information I uncovered of the planned attempt to pilfer the Marie Antoinette handbag? Indeed. I spent much of today in an effort to learn the thief's identity, but without success. Perhaps tomorrow I shall have better fortune." He consulted his timepiece. "Less than half an hour until closing. Let us hope the blackguard waits until the last night of the exhibit to—"

All the lights went out.

The sudden darkness was nearly absolute. There were no street lamps in the immediate vicinity outside the gallery; the only light that penetrated the windows came from the lamps of hacks and carriages passing on Post Street.

A woman's voice cried out in fright. Other voices rose and there was a confused milling about.

Sabina and Charles the Third both reacted immediately. In concert they stepped around the partition and strode to the entrance, where Charles barred it with his body and spread-eagled arms, and shouted in stentorian tones, "Stand clear of the door! No one is allowed to leave!"

Andrew Rayburn's voice also rose querulously out of the darkness: "Remain calm, ladies and gentlemen, remain calm. We will soon have the lights back on."

The others in the room quieted; the milling about ceased. Someone brushed up against Sabina, either by accident or in an attempt to exit; a none too gentle push from Charles the Third brought instant retreat. A match scratched and flared, then a brighter flare came from someone's flint lighter. In the flickering glow the faces of the fifteen or so guests and employees appeared like masks of shadow. Sabina squinted toward the Reticules Through the Ages display. No one was in close proximity to it except the clerk George Eldredge.

The sudden extinguishing of the lights might have been accidental; such blackouts were not uncommon in this new age of electricity. But Sabina distrusted coincidence, the more so when something like this happened. She made her way across the room as rapidly as she was able, her handbag open and her fingers touching the handle of the derringer inside.

She was nearing the ropes that fronted the exhibit when the blackout ended—a period of no more than two minutes after it had begun. But when the lights came on again, George Eldredge's voice rose in a horrified shout.

"The Marie Antoinette bag! It's gone!"

14

SABINA

A babble of shocked exclamations followed the clerk's outcry. Most of the remaining guests were still grouped together in the center of the gallery, all except for Eldredge, who stood pointing tremulously at the display, and Thaddeus Bakker who stood off to one side looking frightened and twitching fingers across the front of his corporation. Even from a distance, Sabina could see that the blue velvet centerpiece case was now empty.

Marcel Carreaux and Andrew Rayburn both ran to the display table. The Frenchman was gesticulating wildly, his saturnine face mottled with a blend of outrage and anxiety; the gallery owner was so pale his face looked as if it had been dusted with talcum powder. Sabina hurried to join them, a sidelong glance telling her that Charles the Third was still guarding the door. No emotion showed on his hawkish countenance. A rattlepate he might be, but he was undeniably calm in a crisis.

She caught hold of Rayburn's arm. "To the front door. Quickly!"

He blinked at her in confusion.

"To lock it. You do have your keys?"

"Yes. Oh, yes, right away." He hurried off, fumbling a ring of keys from his coat pocket.

The Frenchman was beside himself. "The Marie Antoinette, stolen! *Diable! C'est incroyable!*" He turned to Sabina. "Do something, madame. It was your duty to prevent such an outrage—"

"No one could have anticipated the lights going out. Or acted to prevent theft in a blacked-out room full of people."

"But the Marie Antoinette, the Marie Antoinette!" One of Carreaux's flailing hands narrowly missed Sabina's nose. "The gendarmes, the police . . . we must summon them immediately."

"Not just yet, *mon ami.*"

Those words were spoken by Charles the Third, who came striding up with Rayburn at his heels. Carreaux scowled, obviously not recognizing him. "Who are you, m'sieu? Why do you say 'not yet'?"

The crackbrain rattled off half a dozen sentences in rapid French. Sabina could follow just enough of it to become alarmed. Carreaux stared at him, openmouthed. "*That* M'sieu Holmes? No, I do not believe it. The world has been told he is dead—"

Sabina quickly interceded. "And so he is," she said. The glare she directed at Charles the Third plainly said that he soon would be if he persisted. This was no time for him to make his daft pretense known; it would only cause more confusion. "My assistant is inclined to take the similarity in surnames too seriously in times of stress. Isn't that so, *Charles* Holmes?"

There was a small silence. Then he shrugged, and to her relief didn't put forth an argument. "If it pleases you to have it that way. One believes what one chooses to believe."

"One also believes what one sees," Carreaux said in nettled tones. "I see a man dressed in a costume of the streets."

"And for a very good reason which has nothing to do with the present contretemps."

"Contretemps! A thief has made off with the most valuable chatelaine bag in my care and you say only it is a contretemps!"

"Calm yourself, my good fellow. No one has made off with the Marie Antoinette."

"Eh? What's that you say?"

"Mrs. Carpenter and I rushed to the entrance the moment the lights were extinguished and I proceeded to barricade it with my body. No one could possibly have slipped past me."

"Nor did anyone escape through the rear door," Rayburn said. "I entered the storeroom immediately to find out what happened to the lights. A fuse had come loose—I screwed it back in. Then I checked to make certain the door was secure. It was."

"Does anyone other than yourself have a key to it?"

"No. I keep the only one on the ring in my pocket."

"Did anyone else enter the storeroom while you were there?"

"No. Nor could they have afterward without arousing attention. The same is true of my office."

Charles the Third shifted his hawkish gaze to the Frenchman. "So you see, M'sieu Carreaux? Everyone who was in the gallery before the period of darkness is still present. Ergo, both the thief and the missing reticule are still present as well."

"Ah! Yes, this must be so. But who is he and where is the Marie Antoinette?"

"Fear not. The answers to those questions shall not long remain a mystery to Mrs. Carpenter and myself."

Charles the Third seemed bent on taking charge. Sabina did not like the idea of their positions being reversed; such a male-dominant act rankled her as a woman and suffragette as well as the detective hired to protect Reticules Through the Ages. John might have done the same, but at least she knew him well and trusted his judgment. Under different circumstances she would have quickly wrested control from the addlepate, but she had to admit that thus far he had done the right things, asked the right questions, made the right assumptions and decisions. She had already forestalled one potential disruption; there was nothing to be gained in starting another.

Very well, then, let him continue his Sherlockian role for the time being. But if he overstepped himself, or made a false move, she would put an immediate end to his assumed authority—if necessary by boxing his ears or thrusting the muzzle of her derringer under his prominent nose.

The sausage-curled dowager had stepped forward. "Just who are these individuals, Mr. Rayburn?" she demanded. "What gives them the right to take charge of this abominable situation?"

"They're detectives. Mr. Carreaux and I engaged Mrs. Carpenter to provide security for the exhibit. This man is her assistant."

There were murmurs from the assemblage. The gentleman with the pince-nez seemed still to be trying to dislodge an obstruction in his throat; a series of "Harrumph!"'s overrode the other voices. The dowager said in disbelieving tones, "Detectives? A woman and this . . . *this* person?"

"And why not, madam?" Charles the Third asked her.

She sniffed. "You're dressed like a refugee from the Barbary Coast. How can we be sure *you* are not the one who pinched the missing bag?"

A few mutters and grumbles followed this. Sabina, who would have liked to box the dowager's ears as well as those of Charles the Third, sought to reassure everyone that not only was her "assistant" innocent of the theft, but that Carpenter and Quincannon, Professional Detective Services, was the city's most reputable detective agency. One of the guests whom she knew by sight, but whose name she couldn't recall, vouched for the veracity of her statement. Order was then restored, though not for long.

The crackbrain rubbed his hands together briskly. "To repeat my earlier statement, ladies and gentlemen, whoever nicked the chatelaine bag is still in this room. A careful search will turn it up."

A heavyset gentleman in a top hat said, "Do you intend to search each of us?"

"If necessary, sir. Indeed, if necessary."

"Outrageous!" This from the dowager. "I refuse to be treated like a common thief—"

"Whether or not you're a thief, madam, common or otherwise, remains to be determined."

"What? How dare you!"

Once again Sabina hurriedly interceded. "If a search of your person is necessary, it will be done in private and with the utmost prudence. No one will be unduly inconvenienced."

"I, for one, have no objection to being searched," Thaddeus Bakker said. "No innocent person should have."

"Just so, Mr. Bakker."

"Searched by whom?" the dowager said, waving her lorgnette. "These two alleged detectives? Why not the police? Summon the proper authorities, I say."

Charles the Third said, "They shall be once we have both thief and reticule in hand. There is no need for their services at this juncture. Too many cooks spoil the broth, eh?"

"What in heaven's name does that mean?"

He ignored her. "Shall we proceed?" he said.

There were a few more protests, but eventually they all allowed themselves to be herded to the wall behind the food buffet and to remain there in a group. All except Sabina, the crackbrain, Carreaux, and Rayburn, who held a conference some distance away.

"I don't see how searching everyone will turn up the bag," the gallery owner said, nervously stroking his shoelace mustache. "Surely the thief wouldn't have it on his person."

The Frenchman concurred. "*Mais oui.* The clasp alone would make it impossible to conceal."

"Everyone will have to be searched nonetheless," Charles the Third insisted.

"Perhaps the thief has hidden it somewhere in this room, with the intention of returning for it at a later time."

"Or in the storeroom or my office," Rayburn added.

"Not likely in either of those places, Mr. Rayburn. It is a

certainty no one other than you left this room while the lights were out, nor has left it since you turned them on again."

"Yes, that's right."

"We shall conduct our searches of their persons now and have done with that chore first." Charles the Third turned to the Frenchman. "Sooner or later, in one place or another, *M'sieu le conservateur*, we will find the missing article."

"We had better find it," Carreaux said portentously. "If I were to return to Paris without it, I would no longer be assistant *conservateur* at the Louvre Museum."

To be thorough before the searches began, Sabina and Charles the Third probed all possible hiding places in the storeroom and Rayburn's office. They found nothing. Then, while she watched over the women, the crackbrain ushered the male guests, Eldredge, and Holloway into the office, and with Rayburn's help searched each of them. Carreaux apparently insisted that his and Rayburn's persons also be searched and, when that was done, that Charles also submit to a search.

The chatelaine bag remained missing.

Sabina took her turn with the half-dozen women guests, the sausage-curled dowager still angry and making dire threats of a lawsuit against all parties concerned. If a muzzle had been close at hand, Sabina would cheerfully have used it to still her yapping.

None of the women possessed the bag, either.

So it must be hidden somewhere in the gallery. Either by design, in which case the thief believed himself to be more cunning than he was; or because he had realized belatedly that he couldn't get away with the bag and stashed it to avoid being revealed as the guilty party.

Guests and employees were herded into the storeroom, with Carreaux on guard, after which Sabina, Rayburn, and Charles the Third commenced a careful exploration of the gallery. Every possible hiding place was examined—the undersides of the exhibit display table, chairs, the settee by the entrance; the insides of antique vases, jars, and urns; the backs of paintings mounted on the walls; the buffet tables and the food, bottles, plates, and glassware atop them; and every conceivable nook and cranny.

The Marie Antoinette was nowhere to be found.

15

SABINA

"Sacrebleu!" Carreaux exclaimed in exasperation. He had been summoned to join Sabina, Rayburn, and Charles the Third after the gallery search was finished. "You are certain, M'sieu Holmes, that the thief could not have departed during the blackout?"

"Unless he or she has the power to walk through the solid walls, I am. Most assuredly."

"Then why have we not found the Marie Antoinette? No hiding place has been overlooked. *C'est impossible!*"

Charles the Third smiled his enigmatic smile. "So it would seem. But we have eliminated the impossible, and it is an old maxim of mine that when this has been done, whatever remains, however improbable, must be the truth."

"Why do you say we have eliminated the impossible?"

"We have established, have we not, that no one could have left the premises after the theft. Also that the thief could not have hidden the missing reticule anywhere in this or the other rooms. Therefore, as improbable as it might seem, the chatelaine is still in his possession."

"But everyone has been searched. How could the *voleur* still possess it?"

"The answer to that lies in the observation of trifles. The world is full of obvious things which nobody by any chance ever observes."

"Well? What trifles?" Rayburn demanded waspishly.

"Patience, my dear sir. Patience."

"Patience, my foot. Do you know or don't you?"

"I do," Sabina said.

All eyes turned to her. She had been deep in thought; now she was sure she was right in the conclusions she'd drawn from *her* "observation of trifles." Had Charles the Third made the same deduction? No matter. Whether he had or not, the time had come for her to take command.

She said to him, "Do you agree that two individuals, not just one, are involved in the theft?"

Carreaux and Rayburn seemed surprised at the question. The crackbrain showed no reaction; his smile remained enigmatic. "Naturally," he said. "One to loosen the fuse at a prearranged time, the other to step over the rope and lift the reticule from the display table."

"Mr. Rayburn. Is it likely one of the guests would know where the fuse box is located?"

"No. Customers and guests are not allowed in the storeroom." The gallery owner's eyes narrowed. "Are you implying that I—"

"Not at all, sir. You have no credible reason to have stolen the Marie Antoinette."

"One of my clerks then? Holloway, Eldredge?"

"How long has each of them worked for you?"

"Eldredge for four years, Holloway for just under one. But—"

"The storeroom door was not under careful watch, only the display," Sabina said. "One or the other of them could have slipped through unnoticed, loosened the fuse, then hidden himself until after you tightened it to restore the electricity."

Rayburn fussed with his mustache again before he said, "Yes, that's possible. There are places in the storeroom where a man who knows it could briefly hide himself without my seeing him. My attention was on the fuse box when I entered by matchlight, then on returning to the exhibit once the lights were back on."

"Did you notice where Holloway and Eldredge were standing prior to the blackout?"

"Let me think . . . Yes. They were both near the display table, on the side nearest the storeroom door. When the lights came on, Eldredge was in front of the table—apparently the first to notice the Marie Antoinette was missing. He's the one who gave the alarm."

"And Holloway?"

"He was at my side after I stepped out of the storeroom. I remember because he spoke my name."

"Could he have followed you out, walking softly?"

"He could have, yes, if he'd been hiding somewhere near the door."

Martin Holloway was called to join them. The man had a habit of clasping his long-fingered hands at his waist; he stood rubbing them together in an agitated fashion. But his gaze was steady and his posture one of defensive innocence.

He vehemently denied having been in the storeroom. "I was

at the wall next to the display table," he said, "from just before the lights went out until they were restored."

"Who else was near the table prior to the blackout?" Sabina asked.

"George Eldredge. Moving about in front."

"Just him?"

"In the immediate vicinity, yes."

"And you have no idea who snatched the bag?"

"None. None at all."

Over the course of her career Sabina had developed a sharp eye for facial expressions and body movements, a sharp ear for nuances of speech; it was the rare individual who could fool her successfully. She stepped close to the small man, fixed him with her fiercest stare.

"You lie, Mr. Holloway," she said. "I know you're guilty. We all know it. Confess, identify your confederate, and perhaps Monsieur Carreaux will be inclined to be lenient with you."

"But yes, I will," the Frenchman said. "My only concern is the recovery of the Marie Antoinette."

But the clerk foolishly clung to a misguided faith in his partner in crime and his hope for a share of the spoils. "You can't intimidate me," he said. "I had nothing to do with the theft. Nothing, do you hear me? And you can't prove I did."

Sabina said, "I believe we can."

"As do I," Charles the Third concurred.

He escorted Holloway back to wait with the others and returned with George Eldredge, a man some years older and several pounds heavier. Eldredge was cooperative, but had nothing of importance to relate. He had stopped near the far corner of the table when the room went dark, he said, and remained there until the electric lights came on again. He couldn't recall if Holloway had been in the room when he spied the empty blue velvet case; his attention had been riveted on that. Nor could he say who else might have been close enough to step over the ropes and snatch the chatelaine bag in the sudden darkness.

But Sabina could.

She said to Charles the Third, "There's another person to be questioned, and without delay."

"Indeed there is. Will you name him, or shall I?"

That, Sabina thought, may have been because he had made the same final deduction as she, or it may have been a sly bit of face-saving on his part. She was inclined toward the latter. For one thing, while he was proud of his Sherlockian powers of observation, he hadn't spent nearly as much time as she had observing and mingling with the guests the past two nights. And for another, his ego was such that if he did have the answer, he would surely have attempted to seize the moment himself instead of allowing her to do so.

"I will," she said. "Thaddeus Bakker."

"Ah. Yes. Mr. Bakker."

"Fetch him, please."

"You suspect him of being the thief?" Rayburn asked.

"I do."

"But . . . what makes you think so?"

"Because he ate nothing from the buffet last night or prior to the blackout tonight. Because his neck is slender and so are his arms and legs. And because of his frilly white shirt."

The gallery owner gaped at her. "I don't understand."

"You soon will. Now will you please fetch him."

Rayburn did so. Thaddeus Bakker seemed puzzled by the summons; he stood rocking slightly on his heels. "I can't imagine why you asked to see me, Mrs. Carpenter. I know nothing whatsoever about the theft."

"Tell us where you were when the blackout ended."

"Why . . . I don't recall exactly. By the liquor buffet, I believe."

"No, you weren't," Rayburn said. "I saw you standing near the wall beyond the exhibit."

"You must be mistaken—"

"I saw you there as well," Sabina said. "You were just turning around and apparently fussing with your shirtfront. But what you were actually doing was refastening the last of the buttons."

"What of it?" Bakker drew himself up. "Are you suggesting I stole the Marie Antoinette reticule and hid it inside my shirt?"

"Stole the bag, yes. Hid it, yes. But not inside your shirt."

"The accusation is preposterous. I was searched as thoroughly as any of the others."

"Not thoroughly enough. The bag was not and is not in your clothing, Mr. Bakker."

"Then how can you claim I—"

To the astonishment of the other three men, Sabina suddenly and with all her might punched Thaddeus Bakker in his protruding belly.

Her closed fist must have sunk two inches into Bakker's midriff, yet the man's only reaction was a small startled grunt. Thus confirming her suspicions and justifying her bold action.

No genuinely fat man could have absorbed such a violent blow without indications of distress.

Rayburn gasped and Carreaux exclaimed, *"Mon Dieu!"* But Charles the Third understood immediately.

"False!" he cried. "A false corporation!"

Bakker, realizing the game was up, made a clumsy attempt to flee. Charles the Third tripped him, pounced on top, and tore open the man's shirt to reveal exactly what Sabina expected to see—a padded convex mound wrapped in an elasticized garment resembling a woman's corset, a false corporation so cunningly made it would look and feel genuine when the clothing that covered it was searched. The corsetlike garment fit snugly, but not so snugly as to prevent it from being pulled up along one side. Which Charles quickly proceeded to do. A moment later he removed the Marie Antionette from among wads of cotton padding inside.

His bright gaze rested on Sabina as he held the prize up for all to see. "Capital brainwork, my good woman," he said with a hint of jealousy. "And the end game well played!"

A good deal of confusion ensued. Monsieur Carreaux seized the chatelaine bag, examined it, and then, with a Gallic flourish, he threw his arms around Sabina and bestowed moist kisses on each cheek. Charles the Third, with Rayburn's assistance, was busy lifting a weakly struggling Thaddeus Bakker, or whatever his real name was, onto his feet. Some of the guests had spilled out of the storeroom to look on, chattering in excited voices. Martin Holloway, realizing his partner had been captured and the theft ploy foiled, ran to the front door in a panicked effort to escape; Eldredge and the man with the pince-nez restrained him, after which he and Bakker were locked away in Rayburn's office. Eldredge was then sent to summon the police.

It was two hours before the plainclothesmen in charge finished their officious duties and allowed everyone to leave. Two facts resulted from their interrogation of the sullen culprits. Thaddeus Bakker's real name was Horace Binder and he was indeed from Sacramento, where he had been twice arrested and once convicted for jewel robbery. And Martin Holloway was his brother-in-law.

Sabina had little opportunity to speak to Charles the Third while this was going on. He blustered a bit to anyone who would listen, insisting that he was in fact and indeed Sherlock Holmes, "the last and highest court of appeal of detection," and that he, too, had deduced the clever method by which Bakker/Binder had secreted the Marie Antoinette bag. "If my splendid associate had not acted as quickly and in the fashion she did," he said, "I would have done so myself."

Sabina smiled wryly to herself when she overheard this. Horsefeathers, she thought.

When permission was given for them to leave, she sought out Charles the Third, took hold of his arm, and asked if he would mind escorting her home to her flat. He consented gallantly, as she had thought he would. She needed no escort, of course, but she didn't want him slipping away from her again, at least not until she'd had a chance to talk to him privately. Sharing a hansom gave her that opportunity.

Once they were alone together in the cab, he said, "A trying evening, to be sure. But a rather exhilarating one nonetheless.

It is always gratifying to unmask thieves and render them their just deserts."

"Yes, it is."

"Bakker, or Binder, is a clever fellow, but his plan was doomed to failure pitted against not one but two brilliant minds. Once again the observation of trifles and the application of logic have proven my long-held theory that they are the most successful methods of detection."

He paused to produce and light his long, curved clay pipe. Sabina wrinkled her nose; his choice of tobacco was even worse than John's. "I must congratulate you, Mrs. Carpenter," he said then, "on the manner in which you utilized the furniture in your little brain attic tonight. Most detectives on both sides of the Atlantic Ocean, I have found, take in all the lumber of every sort that they come across, so that the knowledge which might be useful to them gets crowded out, or at best is jumbled up with a lot of other things, and they have difficulty in laying hands on it. That is certainly not true of you. Or, for that matter, your erstwhile partner. You are both skillful workmen who are careful, indeed, as to what you take into your brain attics. As of course am I."

Sabina smothered both a sigh and a yawn, and thanked him for the compliment. Then, with deliberate flattery, "You and I do make a rather effective team, don't we?"

"We do indeed."

"Perhaps we can work together again. Assuming, that is, that you plan to remain in San Francisco?"

"At least for the nonce, I do. Though I must return to London fairly soon and ease poor Doctor Watson's mind about the state of my well-being. Meanwhile, I should very much enjoy another commingling of the furniture in our brain attics."

"Tell me, then. Where can I reach you?"

"Why, dear lady, you need only place another newspaper advertisement as you did in this case."

"Yes, but what if I should need to call upon you quickly? And sooner than later? Surely you don't mind revealing your current address to me?"

He was silent for a time, puffing noisily on his pipe, apparently mulling on the advisability of confiding in her. At length he said, "You'll share the information with no one, not even your associate? If the knowledge were to reach the wrong ears, it would have a dire effect on the investigation that required my present disguise."

"You have my word."

"Very well. I am temporarily lodged at a small residential hotel on Stevenson Street."

"Stevenson. That would be Tar Flat."

"I believe that is what the area is called, yes."

Tar Flat was an Irish workingman's neighborhood south of Market, not the sort of place she would have expected Charles the Third to hang his hat. But then he could always be counted on to do the unexpected and often inexplicable. "Which hotel?"

"The Dubliner. Room eleven."

"Under what name?"

"Seamus O'Leary. Though I'm not often to be found there."

"Is there someplace else you can be reached on short notice?"

He hesitated again. Then, "Two blocks south of the hotel there is a pub, or saloon in your American parlance, unimaginatively named the Tam O'Shanter that serves a palatable free lunch as well as alcoholic beverages. It is also the gathering place of certain individuals, thus serving me well as a listening and observation post."

"May I ask why you're staying in Tar Flat?"

"You may ask, but I am not at liberty to answer. Suffice it to say that my presence there is of considerable importance and requires a certain amount of secrecy and subterfuge."

All of this was typical daft blather, though given Charles the Third's past accomplishments, there would be a core of truth in it. Sabina asked, "How long do you expect to be at the Dubliner?"

"I really can't say. At least another week or so. Possibly longer. As you are quite well aware, many investigations require time and cannot be hurried."

"Will you let me know when you move and where?"

"If circumstances permit, dear lady. If circumstances permit."

Sabina let silence descend again for a time. The hack rattled and swayed on the cobblestones, the driver's whip cracking audibly to prod the horse as it drew them up the steep western slope of Russian Hill. The smoke from Charles the Third's pipe had begun to make Sabina feel nauseous; she drew aside the closed side curtain and slid the window open.

As they neared her street, she asked him, "Do you intend to keep your promise about tomorrow?"

"Promise? I recall making no promise."

"But you did. You told me earlier that you would contact Roland Fairchild at the Baldwin Hotel."

"Oh, that. A minor and annoying bit of foolishness, nothing more."

"But you will attend to it? He is, after all, my client."

"Yes, so you said. To locate a person named . . . what was it?"

"Charles Percival Fairchild the Third," Sabina said patiently. "Of Chicago, Illinois. Sole heir to the substantial estate of his deceased father, Charles the Second."

"A euphonious name, but one I had never heard before your mention of it. Nor have I ever been in Chicago, Illinois. But yes, I will pay a call on your client in the morning and set him straight. Is this satisfactory to you?"

"It is."

"Capital. I wish you well in your search for this Charles Percival fellow, wherever he may be."

The hansom drew up in front of Sabina's building. The crackbrain insisted on paying the taxi fare, escorted her to the door, said good night, bowed, and returned to the cab to be whisked away.

Would he pay the call on his cousin in the morning? She could only hope so; she'd done all she could tonight to bring about the meeting. If he failed to appear, she would have no choice but to pursue him in Tar Flat, a rough place for a woman alone, but an even rougher one for a dandified tourist such as Roland W. Fairchild.

She sighed as she keyed open the front door. Unless she received an early communication from one or the other of them, she would have to give up part of her Sunday to find out.

16

QUINCANNON

The proprietor of the Elite Cardroom and Pool Emporium was no respecter of the Sabbath. The place was open bright and early on Sunday morning, which made Quincannon's trip to the neighborhood at least potentially worthwhile. Xavier Jones had still not returned to his boardinghouse. It could be that Cyrus Drinkwater had gotten word to him to lie low after the confrontation with Quincannon yesterday, but that didn't explain Jones's prior absence. In any event, with a little luck he could be eventually tracked down—assuming, of course, that he was still among the living.

The cardroom at the rear of the Elite was empty, but two of the eight pool, snooker, and billiard tables were in use: a pair of young men in rough garb playing a desultory game of snooker, and a middle-aged, nondescript gent practicing cross-bank and combination pool shots by himself. A different oldster manned the cash register this day, a sour-faced fellow wearing a droopy moustache and green-and-gold sleeve garters.

Quincannon asked the same question he'd asked the day

before, and received a loquacious response. Oh, sure, the oldster said, he knew Xavier Jones. No, Jones hadn't been in today. X played cards, not pool—cribbage, mostly, and sometimes whist or poker—but the games didn't usually get started until eleven or so on Sundays on account of some folks went to church first. The clerk aimed a wad of tobacco juice at a spittoon, more or less accurately. Didn't go to church himself, never did hold with organized religion, but that didn't mean he didn't believe in God. Folks worshipped in their own way, and that was the right of it as far as he was concerned. Why, he recollected a miner up Marysville way back in the seventies . . .

"Beg pardon, friend," a voice behind Quincannon said. It belonged to the nondescript gent, he saw when he turned; the man had paused in his practicing and now stood with his hip cocked against his table. "Couldn't help but overhear. Step on over."

Quincannon did as he was bid. "Do you know Xavier Jones?"

"Ought to. I'm a regular here, same as him."

"You wouldn't happen to know where he might be found?"

"Might. My name's Gunderson."

"Quincannon."

"Shoot pool, do you, Mr. Quincannon?"

"Some."

"How about a game while we talk?"

Quincannon had been sizing the fellow up without seeming to. He seemed innocuous enough, friendly, outwardly bored with his solo playing and looking for a bit of companionship. The cue he held negligently in one hand was a house stick. All a pose. Hustler, pool shark—Quincannon had seen enough of them over the years to spot one straightaway.

"Well," he said after a short pause, "I guess I wouldn't mind."

"Straight pool, eight-ball, rotation? Your pleasure."

"Oh, it doesn't matter. Eight-ball?"

"Fine. Lag for break?"

Quincannon nodded his ascent, went to a wall rack to select a cue for himself. A few were slightly warped; he found one that was more or less straight and chalked the tip while Gunderson racked the balls. When they lagged, the shark deliberately stroked his ball into the far rail hard enough so that Quincannon would win the break.

"Looks like we're about evenly matched," Gunderson said. Then, casually, "How about we make it interesting?"

"Interesting?"

"Small wager on the outcome."

"How small?"

"Oh, say five dollars, if that's not too stiff for you?"

Quincannon pretended to think it over. "Well, I don't know . . . Are you sure you may know where I can find Xavier Jones?"

"Sure enough. Tell you about it while we play. Does the wager amount suit you?"

"Well . . . all right. Five dollars."

Gunderson put a five-dollar greenback on the rim of the table; Quincannon matched the amount with a pair of two-and-a-half-dollar gold pieces. His break of the rack was amateurish, dead center on the one-ball so that none of the balls dropped into a pocket.

"Too bad," the shark said. He chalked his cue and sank the eleven ball, giving him stripes, made two more easy shots, then deliberately missed a cross-bank.

Quincannon looked the table over, tapped in the five ball, then feigned bewilderment as to which shot to try next. "About Jones," he said. "He wasn't home this morning and doesn't seem to have been yesterday, either."

"No surprise in that."

"No? Why not?"

"You must not know him very well."

"I don't. My business with him concerns a debt he owes."

"He's got himself a dolly," Gunderson said.

"Ah. You know who she is?"

"Sure thing. Still your shot, friend."

Quincannon missed a corner pocket try at the two ball. Gunderson walked around the table, said, "Looks like you've left me wide open," and proceeded to pocket the rest of the striped balls and then the black eight to win the game. All relatively easy shots, so that he didn't have to reveal the depth of his skill. "My lucky morning," he said then. "But luck can change fast. How about another game, a chance to get even?"

"Maybe. What's Jones's dolly's name?"

"Flora."

"Where does she live?"

"Can't tell you that because I don't know."

"Her last name, then?"

Gunderson produced and lighted a stogie. "I think better when I'm playing, friend. Another game, same stakes?"

"All right."

The shark pocketed his greenback and Quincannon ponied

up a five-dollar coin to join the two quarter eagles. "To show you that I'm a sport," he said, "I'll pass the break to you again."

Quincannon's break was off this time, too, pocketing nothing. Gunderson eyed the table, then cut the twelve ball neatly into a corner pocket—stripes again—and after that dropped the ten ball. Reverse english on the cue ball left him a clean stroke at the fifteen.

"The dolly's last name," Quincannon said as evenly as he could. His patience had begun to run thin.

Down went the fifteen ball. Gunderson sucked at his stogie and released a stream of smoke before he answered. "Delight," he said.

"How's that?"

"Delight. That's her last name. Flora Delight."

"Sounds like a stage name."

The shark lined up and then sank the nine ball on a moderately difficult combination shot. "My eye is better than usual this morning," he said.

Quincannon let that pass. "Stage name, is it? Flora Delight?"

"Sure. Nobody ever born with one like it."

"Where does she perform?"

Gunderson made his next shot with ease, said, "Eight ball in the side," and promptly ended the game. "My lucky day, for a fact," he said. "I'm not usually this accurate." Then, casually, "I don't suppose you'd be interested in one more game?"

"If you'll tell me where Flora Delight performs and what it is she does," Quincannon said. "And if you'll give me a chance to win my money back and your fiver along with it."

Gunderson tried not to show how much he liked that suggestion, but the gleam of avarice shone in his eyes. "Double the stakes? Why, sure, friend, I'll oblige you," he said. Then, as he racked the balls, "The Variety Gay, on Stockton. Cancan and buck-and-wing dancer, afternoon and evening shows. Hot stuff, according to Jones."

"Sundays included?"

"Seven days a week."

Quincannon laid twenty dollars in greenbacks on top of the previous stakes. "You mind if I break again?"

"Not at all."

Quincannon chalked his cue, set the cue ball in position. When he broke the rack this time, it was with a perfectly placed stroke that dropped the one ball cleanly. He eyed the table and then proceeded to run it, swiftly and methodically, finishing up with a long cut on the eight into a corner pocket. Then he laid down the cue, scooped up his winnings, said "*My* lucky day, friend," to the slack-jawed shark who would never know that he'd spent hundreds of hours in Hoolihan's and elsewhere holding his own against some of the city's best pool and billiard players, and walked out of the Elite whistling a temperance tune.

The Variety Gay was a typical Barbary Coast melodeon, of the sort which featured a collar-and-elbow variety show— bawdy songs and comedy skits, and scantily clad dancers. One of the older and cheaper houses; an ancient mechanical reed organ, the instrument from which the name melodeon had derived, was still in evidence, though now as nothing more than a decoration; it had been supplanted by a modern honky-tonk piano currently being played by a sweating fat man in accompaniment to one of the skits. At tables and in boxes the all-male audience—the only women allowed in such places were the waitresses and performers—was early Sunday afternoon sparse, the laughter from the dozen or so customers desultory. Even at this hour, layers of tobacco smoke hung in the room and the atmosphere was odious with the stale smells of beer, wine, and the cheap perfume worn by the serving and dancing girls.

Quincannon stood for a few seconds, breathing through his mouth while he scanned the men. Two or three matched the description he had of Xavier Jones. He made his way to a table midway along, and was immediately pounced upon by one of the several waitresses who sold drinks on commission—a plump, nearly bare-bosomed girl whose skirts ended almost at her knees. None of her displayed attributes held his eye; she would have been slightly more appealing, in fact, if they had been fully covered up.

He ordered a beer, which he had no intention of drinking, and when she brought it he asked, "Do you know a gent named Xavier Jones? Friend of Miss Flora Delight."

She eyed him suspiciously. "Why're you asking?"

"I was told he might be here. I have some money for him."

"That so?" The suspicion had quickly given way to greedy interest. "How about some for me? He don't need it, but I sure do."

"You do know him, then. Is he here now?"

She held out her hand. In addition to a dime for the beer, Quincannon filled it with a fifty-cent piece. This seemed to satisfy her.

"Most nights and some afternoons," she said. "He's got a real big crush on Flora, always buying her flowers and trinkets. Champagne, too, can you believe it? She can't, hardly."

"Which one is he?"

"Gent up front there, with the glass of wine." The waitress leaned forward, revealing even more of her freckled bosom, and said chummily, "You wouldn't like to buy a girl some champagne, would you? Later on, I mean, somewheres else. She'd be awful grateful if you did."

"A tempting offer, but I'm a married man with five children."

"That don't matter none to me."

"I also have an unfortunate social disease."

"That does," she said, and made a rapid departure.

The skit on stage ended with a borderline obscene joke and a final tinny riff on the piano, to a smattering of applause. The piano player shuffled off into the wings, and a gaudily dressed gent came out to announce a brief intermission. The stage lights dimmed then, deepening the smoky gloom in the rest of the room. Quincannon stood, went to the table where Xavier Jones was sitting, drew out a chair and parked himself in it.

Jones turned his head, frowning. He wasn't such-a-much: medium-sized, balding, his thin-lipped mouth partially concealed by brown mustaches waxed at the ends. He wore a suit and tie, the only man in the Variety Gay besides Quincannon who did.

"Hello, Xavier. Waiting for your dolly's next specialty number?"

"What the hell do you mean, dolly?"

"Flora. Unless you have more than one."

"I never seen you before, mister. What do you know about Flora and me?"

"I know she's a Delight. And that you buy her flowers, trinkets, and champagne and spend a good deal of time watching her perform and in her company afterward. Which is one reason you're such a hard man to find, though mayhap not the only one."

"Who the devil are you? What do you want?"

"Otto Ackermann's steam beer formula and Elias Corby, among other things."

Jones's jaw unhinged like a puppet's. He went board stiff in his chair. "Christ Almighty," he said.

"No, John Quincannon. A name you recognize, I'll wager."

". . . I don't know nothing about what happened at Golden State."

"We both know that's not true."

"I don't have to talk to you," Jones said, and started to stand up.

Quincannon caught his coat sleeve and yanked him back down. At the same time, with his other hand, he opened his coat to reveal the handle of his Navy Colt. "You'll talk to me if you value your hide."

"You wouldn't dare draw that sidearm in here—"

"Wouldn't I?" Quincannon smiled his predatory smile. "I can unholster it fast as a lightning strike, crack you over the head, and holster it again without anybody noticing, then haul you up and carry you out to the alley where you'll talk when you wake up or suffer a variety of other meannesses. Put me to the test if you believe I'm bluffing."

In the smoky, lamplit gloom Jones's eyes were shadowed, but

his fear-rippled expression was plain enough; so was the fact that he seemed to be making an effort to swallow his Adam's apple. "I don't believe you're bluffing," he said.

"Smart lad. Now then. Sit calm, answer my questions truthfully, and I'll leave you to watch Flora's next number. Fair enough?"

"Just . . . walk away? That's all you'll do?"

"That's all. There's no need for the coppers unless you give me trouble."

"I don't want no trouble with you or anybody else, least of all the police."

"We'll get along then," Quincannon said. "First question. Where is the formula?"

"I don't know."

"Bunkum. What did you do with it after it was turned over to you?"

Jones licked his lips, not meeting Quincannon's eyes. His gaze kept flicking to the Navy, as if it might jump out of the holster of its own volition and bite him like a snake.

"You gave it to the man on whose orders you were acting, didn't you. Your employer, Cyrus Drinkwater."

"No. No, it was my idea to, ah, get the recipe. Mr. Drinkwater, he didn't know nothing about it."

"Bunkum," Quincannon said again, more sharply this time. "The theft was his idea, not yours. And you passed the formula on to him. The truth now—I take a dim view of lies and evasions."

". . . All right. But if he finds out—"

"He won't find out, not from me as long as you keep giving straight answers. What did he do with it?"

"Put it in his safe."

Quincannon sighed inaudibly. He'd been afraid that would be the case. "At West Star?"

"No. In his office downtown."

"Still there, so far as you know?"

Jones gave a jerky head bob.

"Did you make a copy?"

"No. Wasn't any need."

"Did he?"

"Not that I know about."

"So then you've yet to make use of it at West Star."

"That's right. Still brewing with our old formula. Mr. Drinkwater . . . he said it was too soon, we should wait a while."

"Good advice. See that you follow it," Quincannon said. And when Jones bobbed his head again in agreement, "Now then. Elias Corby. Where can I find him?"

"I don't know. I never had nothing to do with Corby."

"Remember my warning about lies, Xavier? Corby and Caleb Lansing worked in cahoots to steal the recipe—that's a fact and I can prove it. It's also a fact that they murdered Otto Ackermann, then Corby murdered Lansing—"

"Murder! No, listen, all I did was recruit Lansing and pay him off. He's the one brought Corby into it. Ackermann wasn't supposed to get hurt, nobody was. Them damn fools—"

"Where's Corby now?"

"I told you, I don't have no idea where he is. I hardly know him, only saw him a couple of times."

"Does he have a dolly, too, one he spends his money on?"

"I don't know. He never said nothing if he does."

"Did he say anything about what he intended to do with his share of the payoff?"

"No. Not to me." Then, as if struck by a memory, "But once Lansing said something about a farm . . ."

"About Corby and a farm?"

"That's right. Some farm owned by a widow he knows that he was thinking of buying."

"Located where?"

"I don't remember. Upcountry someplace."

"Upcountry covers a good deal of territory."

"Not too far away. Lansing said Corby'd been up there and back in the same day."

The piano player had returned; he tinkled the ivories, then erupted into a tinny rendition of a cancan number. Out came half a dozen high-kicking dancers in long skirts, petticoats, and black stockings, to applause and wolf whistles from the small crowd. One of them must have been Flora Delight; in spite of the pressure Quincannon had put him under, Jones's head swung toward the stage and his gaze held there.

Ah, love and lust. Even more powerful emotions than fear— temporarily, anyhow.

Quincannon got to his feet. He was done with Jones for the nonce, and his memory had disgorged a possible lead to the location of the upcountry farm. He made a swift exit from the Variety Gay, leaving the lovestruck dolt still gazing raptly at his heart's Delight.

17

QUINCANNON

Two middle-aged women dressed in their Sunday finery were blocking the stoop to Elias Corby's boardinghouse. Gossiping about a neighbor, from the segment of their conversation Quincannon caught as he walked up. "Good afternoon, ladies," he said, doffing his hat.

They responded in kind, though it was plain that they begrudged the interruption of their tittle-tattle.

"Pleasant Sunday weather, wouldn't you agree?"

"I wouldn't," one of them said. "Too much wind, not enough sun."

"Indeed. If you'll excuse me . . ." He started past them to the stairs.

"Here, now," the other woman said, "you're not familiar to me, sir. Visiting or a new tenant?"

"Oh, I've been here before. More than once."

"That doesn't quite answer my question—"

"Indeed," he said, smiled, doffed his hat again, and proceeded jauntily to the door. Behind him, the women resumed their conversation in lowered voices. Gossiping again, probably about him now.

The upstairs hallway was deserted. He had no difficulty picking the lock on Corby's door for the third time; in fact he'd become so adept at it that he was through the door and inside in something under twenty seconds. A quick look through the two rooms assured him that everything was as it had been when he'd accosted and arrested the murderous bookkeeper. The fact that he'd then failed to hold on to Corby after having failed to yaffle Lansing, through no fault of his either time, still galled him. And would until Corby was once more in his clutches, with all possible safeguards in place against another escape.

It was the calendar that hung on the parlor wall, noticed but not closely examined on his first visit, that had brought him here. The name of the Los Alegres firm that it advertised was Pioneer Hatchery, purveyors of "grade-A single-comb leghorn chicken eggs and other fine poultry products." The illustration, done in photographic style, was of a giant egg labeled Pioneer; a smiling man stood possessively beside it, and several chickens, presumably single-comb leghorns, pecked in the foreground.

The facing page was of the present month, February, and the present year. Nothing had been written on it. Quincannon took it down and turned it over. Nothing on the back, either. He riffled through the pages. January was also blank; so were March and April. Ah, but May wasn't. One date, the seventeenth, bore a notation in ink in Corby's neat bookkeeper's hand.

Ella's birthday.

Ella. The widowed owner of a farm in Los Alegres or vicinity? The calendar sent by her to Corby, or obtained by him on a visit to her?

Quincannon flipped through the rest of the pages. All of them were blank. Pioneer Hatchery's address was on the calendar; he copied it down in his notebook.

On his way out he reviewed what he knew of Los Alegres. It was most definitely an upcountry town, located some forty miles north of the city. Founded in the 1830s by General Mariano Vallejo, then commandant of the San Francisco Presidio, as a summer home on his sprawling Mexican land grant. In the years since, it had evolved into a thriving community of some twenty-five hundred souls, known for poultry processing and grain milling. Eggs were its primary industry; more than half the eggs shipped to San Francisco came from Los Alegres.

The town itself had been built along the banks of a wide saltwater estuary, a riverlike waterway that wound through tule marshes to San Pablo Bay. That body of water was directly connected to San Francisco Bay, thus making it easy and profitable for large amounts of eggs, poultry, dairy products, hay, hides, produce, and other goods to be shipped to the city from Sonoma County, in exchange for grain and feed, lumber, hardware, and equipage.

Quincannon had been there only once, having made the trip for business purposes on one of the paddlewheel passenger steamers that plied the estuary along with flat-bottom barges and dredgers that kept its shallow, muddy bottom free of buildups of silt. This was the most direct route to Los Alegres, but also the slowest. The faster option was by way of ferry to

Sausalito, then by train on the San Francisco and North Pacific line.

It was no short trip either way, and the evidence that the widow's farm was where Corby had gone to ground was flimsy at best. Still, he had no other leads; no message had been forthcoming from any of his informants. And if the name Ella did belong to the widow, he ought to be able to locate the farm with relative ease once he arrived in Los Alegres.

As usual on Sundays the Ferry House at the foot of Market Street was teeming with departing and arriving passengers, luggage carts, porters, and a variety of vendors hawking their wares. The old wooden building had already begun to undergo renovation into the city landmark it was intended to become—a new Ferry Building, as it was to be called, with a sandstone façade, an ornamental 245-foot-tall clock tower modeled after one in Seville, Spain, a 660-foot skylit, two-story concourse on the second floor which would provide access to the ferries, marble walls and decorative mosaic marble floor, crossed lattice windows, and other architectural wonders. Quincannon was all in favor of the refurbishment; the present structure was much too small and cramped to properly accommodate the ever-increasing number of travelers.

As he made his way through the throng inside, on a zigzag course to the information booth, he heard his name called. He stopped in mild surprise, turned to see a round, graying man of some sixty years striding toward him. A smile of pleasure parted his freebooter's beard when he recognized the gent's bulbous nose (which someone had once likened to a keg of whiskey with a swollen bung), the habitual Havana cigar jutting from a corner of his mouth, and the equally habitual butternut suit and square-crowned hat.

"Well—Mr. Boggs! A sight for sore eyes."

"I'll say the same for you, my boy."

They shook hands warmly. Boggs was head of the San Franciso field office of the Secret Service, housed in the U.S. Mint at Fifth and Mission streets; had in fact been one of thirty detectives who had been brought together to form the Service in 1865, and was a personal friend of William P. Wood, its first chief, who had handpicked him for his position here. He was also Quincannon's former boss, mentor, and friend of long standing.

When a stray bullet from Quincannon's pistol fired during a running gun battle with a gang of Arizona counterfeiters had accidentally struck and killed a pregnant woman and her unborn child, he had sought to drown his lingering guilt in liquor. It was Boggs who had ignored the Service's rules by allowing him to remain on the government payroll, thus saving him from a descent into drunken debasement that would likely have ended his life. No one had been happier when Quincannon finally made peace with his conscience, largely through his connection with Sabina, and taken the pledge upon quitting the Service to begin his new career as the city's foremost private investigator.

"Where have you been keeping yourself?" Boggs asked. "It has been quite a while since I've seen you."

"Busy, as always. But no busier than you, I'll hazard."

"And so I'll be as long as I'm alive and counterfeiters continue to ply their misbegotten trade."

"You'll be at your desk at age one hundred, then."

"Hah. Little enough chance of that. Where are you bound today?"

"Sonoma County, if I can arrange passage. On the trail of a thief and murderer."

"The Golden State brewery business? I saw your name mentioned in the newspapers in connection with it."

"None other."

"Where in Sonoma County do you think your man is?"

"Los Alegres or vicinity."

"Ah. If you have need of official assistance, Lincoln Evans, the town constable, will provide it. I had occasion to work with him on a government case a while back. Knows his onions and honest as they come. His office is in the city jail on Fourth Street."

"I'll remember that, thanks."

"You'll get your man in any event, I'm sure."

"I always do, sooner or later. You taught me well, Mr. Boggs."

"I take no credit," Boggs said gruffly. Praise always embarrassed him. "You were born with the right stuff, John. Polished off the rough edges yourself, as any good man should. Well, I'd best be on my way. My ferry's due to depart shortly."

"Where are you off to?"

"Oakland. Sunday dinner with my daughter and her family. Damn nuisance, these fatherly duties."

Bosh. Boggs doted on his daughter and his grandson.

"My regards to Eleanor."

"And mine to your partner. A fine figure of a woman, Mrs. Carpenter. Anything of a romantic nature in your relationship yet?"

"Not yet. But I'll succeed in that quest sooner or later, too. I always bag my woman as well as my man."

Boggs chuckled. "Good luck, my boy. Drop around to my office one day soon. We'll have lunch and tell each other lies about our professional escapades."

"I will," Quincannon said, and meant it. "But the stories won't be lies."

Another handshake, and Boggs hurried off to catch his ferry.

Quincannon continued to the information booth, where he was told that the last of the two Sunday steamers to Los Alegres had left forty minutes before. The next one for Sausalito was scheduled to leave in half an hour. If he took passage on it, he would arrive in time to make a connection with the day's final northbound SF&NP passenger train. But this meant he would have to travel without luggage, in nothing more than the clothes on his back. And since the train wouldn't arrive in Los Alegres until six o'clock, it would be too late to begin his inquiries.

He was a fastidious man, and the prospect of spending a night and at least one day in an upcountry farm town without such necessities as changes of clothing and underwear, brushes, comb, and his beard-trimming scissors, held no appeal whatsoever. Far better that he should take the fastest route north first thing in the morning. He booked early passage on the Sausalito ferry and the SF&NP train, which if they were both on schedule would put him in Los Alegres shortly past noon.

The delay was meaningless, really. If Elias Corby was holed

up at the farm of a widow named Ella, he would still be there twenty-four hours hence. Quincannon's father had served with Allan Pinkerton during the Civil War, and in addition to learning from him many investigative techniques that he'd utilized himself and passed on to his son, he'd taken to quoting some of his favorite axioms. One of which was that a manhunter functions at his keenest after a good night's sleep in his own bed.

With that in mind, Quincannon hied himself first to Hoolihan's, where he filled the hollow in his stomach, and then rode a cable car home to follow Allan Pinkerton's sage advice.

18

SABINA

The last person she expected to come knocking on her door on a Sunday morning was a uniformed policeman she'd never seen before.

It was nearing eleven o'clock and she was about to leave for church, after which she intended to lunch with cousin Callie and then call on Roland W. Fairchild to find out if Charles the Third had kept his promise. When she opened the door to be confronted by the bluecoat, her first thought was that his presence had something to do with the previous night's hubbub at the Rayburn Gallery. But he soon disabused her of that notion.

"Officer Dundee, Mrs. Carpenter," he said with cap in hand but no smile on his beefy countenance. "I've been sent to fetch you. If you'll come with me, please."

Past him she could see a police van waiting at the curb, with a second bluecoat standing beside it. "Come with you where?" she asked. "The Hall of Justice?"

"No, ma'am."

"Where, then?"

"You'll soon see. Come along, now. Lieutenant McGinn is waiting."

Her brow furrowed. "I don't know a Lieutenant McGinn. What does he want with me?"

"That's not for me to say. He'll tell you himself."

Sabina had no choice but to go along. As the van clattered them downhill toward the city center, she tried again to pry information out of Officer Dundee, but he remained stoically silent. The feeling of alarm in her grew as they turned east on Market Street, and became full-fledged when she saw that their destination was the Baldwin Hotel and that two other police vehicles were on the circular carriageway at the front entrance, one parked and the other just about to leave. That one she recognized as the coroner's morgue wagon.

Oh, Lord! Not Charles the Third!

The van rattled to a stop behind the morgue wagon. A knot of onlookers were being kept at a distance by more bluecoats, Sabina saw as she alighted with Dundee at her side. Among them were a number of reporters from the city's half-dozen newspapers; one of them, she was sorry to note, was that dreadful muckraking, backbiting columnist for the *Evening Bulletin,* Homer Keeps.

Dundee escorted her inside, across the mostly empty lobby, and into one of the elevators. They ascended and stopped at the third floor, then proceeded down the hall to room 311. Dundee knocked, and when a gruff voice responded, gave his name and said he'd accomplished his mission. The door was opened by a young, grim-visaged stranger with notebook and pencil in hand, obviously a plainclothes detective, who appraised Sabina briefly before stepping aside. She steeled herself as they entered.

A large, gray-haired man of some fifty years stood in the middle of the room, his thumbs hooked in his vest pockets. He wore a rumpled suit and a tie either carelessly knotted or pulled askew; a watch chain with the largest elk's-tooth fob she'd ever seen was draped across his middle. His eyes were shrewd but on the dull side—the unimaginative plodding sort, she guessed. She had never seen him before, either, but he was even more obviously a police detective; she would immediately have identified him as such if she'd spied him in the midst of a crowd in Union Square.

Behind him, Octavia Fairchild was seated on the tufted red plush settee, her large-boned body encased in a plum-colored silk dressing gown. There was nothing haughty about her today. She sat with shoulders bowed, her hands in her lap twisting a lace handkerchief; tears stained her cheeks, and the left one bore a blood-caked gash some two inches long. The look she gave Sabina was one of grief and suppressed anger, but lacking any of the malice of their previous meeting.

There was no one else in the room. But others had been here recently, one of them the occupant of the departed morgue wagon. The overturned chair before the hearth, and the still fresh bloodstains spattered on the carpet next to it, made this all too plain.

The gray-haired detective said in his gruff voice, "You're Mrs. Sabina Carpenter? Good. Police Lieutenant McGinn."

"Why was I brought here, Lieutenant? What happened?"

"Murder, that's what happened," Octavia Fairchild said in a strained, tremulous voice. "Foul murder."

"Who was killed?"

"Who do you suppose? My husband, poor Roland. Viciously slain in cold blood—"

"That'll do, Mrs. Fairchild," McGinn said, not unkindly. Then, to Sabina, "You were summoned to help us catch the man who committed the crime. The man you were hired by the victim to locate, Charles Fairchild."

Sabina had felt a small relief when the victim was identified as her client; rather him than Charles the Third. But now she felt only bewilderment. "Why would he murder his cousin?"

"He came to see Mr. Fairchild this morning. At your direction after that business at the Rayburn Gallery last night, according to what he told the victim. Is that right?"

"Yes. I talked him into it, as per my client's wishes. But Charles was perfectly amiable about it. He seemed to bear no ill will toward his cousin."

"The evidence says he bore plenty. Doesn't believe he's Charles Fairchild, got some screws loose and thinks he's this British detective, Sherlock Holmes. Showed up here at . . . what time, Hatton?"

The younger detective consulted his notebook. "Ten-fifteen. Dressed in what he called his 'true colors' and carrying a walking stick with a heavy knob."

True colors. That meant Inverness cape, deerstalker cap, blackthorn stick—the outfit he'd worn the first time Sabina had met him.

"Insisted he was this Holmes gent," McGinn said, "and that he'd never heard of Charles Fairchild, never been to Chicago, and had no intention of going there. Victim tried to talk sense to him, but he wasn't having any. Started yelling that the victim was trying to . . . what was the word he used?"

"Persecute," Hatton said.

"Trying to persecute him and he wouldn't stand for it. Then without warning he up and bashed Mr. Fairchild over the head with his stick."

"Kept hitting Roland with it!" Octavia Fairchild cried. "Hitting and hitting him even after he fell!"

"Skull crushed in four places," Hatton said.

"When I screamed he spun around and struck me a glancing blow." She touched the cut on her cheek. "If I hadn't ducked away and continued screaming, he would have killed me, too!"

"Did your husband do anything to provoke the attack?" Sabina asked her. "Push or strike him, perhaps?"

"Of course not! Roland was not a violent man."

"Neither is Charles the Third, in my experience."

"You have only had limited dealings with him, you admitted that to me when you were here before. You have no idea what that madman is capable of. I do because I witnessed it!"

McGinn gave her a look and she subsided, sniffling. "Mrs. Fairchild's screams drove him out. He managed to get clear of the hotel before any of the staff knew what happened. The house dick searched the neighborhood and so did my men when they arrived. No sign of him."

Sabina said slowly, "And you think I might know where he can be found."

"Stands to reason. He was with you the past two nights at the art gallery, so you must've tracked him down."

"But I didn't. He came to the gallery the first night in answer to a personals advertisement I placed in the newspapers."

"He tell you or give you any idea where he's lodging?"

Sabina begged the question by saying, "He was questioned by the investigating officers last night. Surely they asked for his present address."

"They did, and he gave them one."

"Well, then—"

"This one," McGinn said. "The Baldwin Hotel."

Shrewd and slyly playful, as always. Daft, yes, but a man of keen intelligence not unlike that of the famous detective he believed himself to be—a cerebral individual devoted to solving crimes, not the witless sort who committed them. It seemed out of character, real or fancied, for him to resort to sudden violent behavior. Unless he'd been severely provoked or threatened, as may well have been the case in the death of Artemas Sneed last fall. If he had killed the blackmailer then, the deed had been almost certainly one of self-defense. And Sneed had been skewered with a sword cane, which Charles's stick likely was, not bashed on the head with it several times in a blind rage . . .

"Well, Mrs. Carpenter?" the lieutenant said. "*Do* you know where we can find the man?"

All her professional instincts commanded that she give McGinn the names of the Dubliner Hotel and Tam O'Shanter pub in Tar Flat. And yet it seemed almost an act of betrayal to do so without knowing Charles's side of what had taken place here this morning. It was difficult to imagine him bludgeoning his cousin to death in a homicidal frenzy, but if he had, he must have been driven to it in some way. Would he perhaps attack her in a similar fashion if she questioned him about it? No. Of that much she felt certain; he had never been anything except courtly and respectful to her. Would he admit to the crime and reveal the reason? He might; she had never known him to tell an outright lie. In that event she could and would act accordingly.

"No, Lieutenant," she said, one of the few willful lies she'd ever told, "I'm afraid I don't."

McGinn finally permitted her to leave. Octavia Fairchild was weeping again by then, saying between sobs, "I can't bear the thought of that monster escaping punishment for what he did to my poor Roland. You must find him—you must!" The woman's expressions of grief and outrage seemed genuine enough, but they struck Sabina as exaggerated, overly dramatic. From what she had observed of the Fairchilds' union, it had been something considerably less than idyllic.

The bluecoat, Dundee, with McGinn's permission, offered to provide return transport to her lodgings. Under different circumstances, Sabina might have declined. But home was where she needed to go now, and the police van would get her there just as quickly as a cab. As John was fond of saying, why pay for what you can have free of charge?

When they exited the elevator, she saw to her dismay that the gaggle of newshounds had been permitted to enter the lobby. And naturally the first of them to notice her was Homer

Keeps. The nasty little muckraker accosted her before she and Dundee could escape.

"Ah, Mrs. Carpenter," he said around the cigar clamped between his yellowing teeth. His piggish little eyes glittered eagerly. "A statement for the press, if you please."

"I don't please." She attempted to move past him, but he scurried around Dundee to block her way again.

"Why were you brought here in a police van? What have you to do with the crime that took place here this morning?"

The bluecoat answered for her. "The lady's not at liberty to give out any statements to the press."

"Does it have anything to do with the attempted theft at the Rayburn Gallery last night?"

"As the officer just told you," Sabina said, "I'm not at liberty to comment."

The other newshounds were now grouped around Keeps. One of them started to ask a question of his own, but the fat little mudslinger overrode him. "Who is the weirdly outfitted gent who assisted you in the apprehension of the handbag thieves, the one who calls himself Sherlock Holmes? Does *he* have anything to do with the murder of the hotel guest?"

"All questions you should be asking Lieutenant McGinn," Dundee said.

"That I will. That I will. But now I'm asking them of Mrs. Carpenter, and as a representative of the fourth estate I demand satisfaction." A long ash fell from his cigar onto the front of his frock coat, joining the residue of numerous others that he hadn't bothered to brush off. "You and your none too respectable partner have a serious history, serious indeed, of participation in all sorts of scurrilous crimes—"

"Most of which we've solved or helped solve to the satisfaction of all concerned."

"Not all. Oh, no, not all. The people have a right to know the truth, the whole truth, of these latest heinous acts of violence and chicanery."

"Yes, they do," Sabina agreed. "These and all others that plague our city. But they'll never learn the truth of anything whatsoever by reading Homer Keeps's columns in the *Evening Bulletin*."

The other reporters laughed. Keeps spluttered indignantly, his round face reddening. Dundee shouldered past him, ushered Sabina out of the hotel and into the waiting van with no further harassment.

In her rooms, she rummaged in the trunk she used for storage of various odds and ends. She couldn't very well make a sojourn into Tar Flat dressed as she was in her rather expensive Sunday best. Or in any clothing that would make her an object of attention in that neighborhood. Charles the Third may have fled the city by now, but she doubted it. If he was guilty of Roland Fairchild's murder, he was not the sort of man to panic and Tar Flat was as safe a haven as any. If he was innocent, he would have returned there to continue his mysterious surveillances.

From the trunk she took the outfit she wore for outdoor activities such as biking, picnicking, and hiking—a plain skirt and a nondescript shirtwaist. Two other trunk items completed her wardrobe: a cloth handbag into which her derringer fit nicely, and an out-of-date, daisy-decorated bonnet that she had bought on a whim and neglected to discard even though it made her look just a bit dowdy.

Looking at herself in the full-length bedroom mirror, she decided she would past muster in Tar Flat. She also had the wry thought that the costume amounted to a disguise. Hardly as outlandish as any of those Charles the Third was so fond of, but a disguise nonetheless. In a manner of speaking, she was now employing one of the crackbrain's favorite gambits.

19

SABINA

Tar Flat had gotten its name from the neighborhood's main industry, the Donahues' gas works at the corner of First and Howard streets. The plant had been distilling coal to manufacture illuminating gas since the early fifties, and its originally primitive method of distillation at low temperatures had resulted in great quantities of sludge waste that were disposed of into open tidewater at the eastern edge of the compound. The sludge destroyed shellfish and the industry that harvested them, and the foul, tarry stench that ensued provided the nickname. In recent years better technology had put an end to the dumping, much of the sludge had been removed, and the smell had slowly dissipated. Now, fortunately, it was all but gone.

Most of Tar Flat's inhabitants lived west of First Street, in the three blocks south of Market. Numerous houses lined the main streets and narrower byways that divided the blocks in half. Most of the dwellings were small, a few taller and larger with balconies and fire escapes, many with single-room backyard units that housed unmarried workers and family relatives. Saloons proliferated, along with dozens of small shops—grocers, fruit-sellers, bakers, barbers, plumbers, tailors, furniture and clothing retailers. Packed in among the commercial buildings were the boardinghouses and residential hotels such as the Dubliner.

Sabina made her way along Sunday-crowded sidewalks, dodging shrieking children and a horse-car that made a careless turn and nearly mowed her down. Some of the close-packed wooden buildings flanking Stevenson Street showed signs of neglect and decay. If a fire were ever to erupt here, it would spread rapidly, the devastation would be catastrophic, and not a few lives would be lost.

The Dubliner Hotel was one of the taller buildings, a paint-peeling, two-story clapboard affair with a small sign over the front door. The lobby was not much larger than an alcove, a short reception desk half hidden under a staircase and presided over by a slat-thin elderly man. He put down the newspaper he'd been reading and peered at Sabina through thick-lensed glasses as she crossed to the desk.

"A good afternoon to you, missus," he said in a brogue as thick as molasses. His smile revealed the absence of two molars and an incisor.

"Good afternoon. Would Mr. Seamus O'Leary be in his room?"

"That he's not. Went out again, he did, some time ago."

"So he's been in and out more than once today?"

"Twice. Away early this mornin', back just past the noon hour, away again a few minutes later."

"Did you happen to notice anything unusual about him when he returned at noon?"

"Unusual, missus?"

"As if he might have been in a fight or accident. Blood on his hands, face, or clothing."

The elderly Irishman cocked an eyebrow. "And why would ye be asking such as that?"

"He sometimes gets into a scrap when he's had a wee bit too much to drink. He's my uncle, you see."

"Ah, now I do. Ye needn't worry. 'Twasn't a speck of blood on Mr. O'Leary, nor his duds mussed."

"Was he carrying his blackthorn stick?"

"When he first went off? Aye, and wearing his Inverness cape over his Sunday best. Bound for church then, he was, I'm guessin'."

If only he had been!

"Was he dressed the same when he went out again, or had he changed clothing?"

"Changed. Had on that, ah, peculiar coat of his with the fancy red collars. Ye know the one, surely."

Sabina nodded. The same long-tailed broadcloth with the red velvet collars he'd worn at the gallery last night. "Was he carrying anything with him?" she asked.

"His fiddle."

"Fiddle?"

"Aye. And a fair hand he is with it, too, if a mite squawky at times." As usual Charles the Third was full of surprises, large and small. Sabina had never heard him play the fiddle, but she had heard him playing the violin at Dr. Axminster's home during the course of the Bughouse Affair. "A mite squawky" was an apt description of his prowess with stringed instruments.

"Is that all he carried with him?" she asked. "No carpetbag or other luggage?"

"Naught but the fiddle. Did ye be expectin' him to?"

"Well, he sometimes moves from one place to another on a whim."

" 'Tisn't plannin' to move out so far's I know."

"Did he happen to say where he was off to?"

"That he didn't. But like as not you'll be finding him at the Tam O'Shanter pub two blocks down. Does his fiddling there, I'm told, when he ain't doing it here in his room."

Sabina thanked him and took her leave, her concern somewhat eased. The four crushing blows to Roland Fairchild's skull would surely have spattered some blood on the wielder of the stick. Still, the elderly clerk's testimony that Charles the Third was blood-free on his return from the Baldwin Hotel was by no means definite; those thick-lensed glasses he wore testified to poor eyesight. The fact that Charles had departed with fiddle instead of luggage in hand indicated he meant to continue to stay at the Dubliner, but that, too, was open to question.

She found her way through the teeming streets to the Tam O'Shanter. Like most of the saloons in Tar Flat, it had a nondescript façade with a half-shaded window next to the entrance to prevent passers-by from peering inside—a typical workingman's watering hole. The sounds of male voices raised in song came from within. She hesitated at the door. She had never been in a saloon such as this, but she knew what to expect from the patrons when she entered. Respectable ladies shunned such resorts; the few members of her sex who didn't were either slovenly alcoholics or women of easy virtue whose favors were available to one and all.

The song that was being lustily sung by a small group of men at the far end of a plain plank bar, something about a Tipperary Bull, continued when Sabina entered, but several other pairs of eyes turned in her direction and remained fixed on her. She stood aloof and expressionless, scanning the bare room with its thick pall of tobacco smoke and strong odors of Irish whiskey and beer. There were some two-score customers seated at a scattering of puncheon tables or spread along the bar. All were men except for a pair of middle-aged slatterns hunched together at a corner table.

The dim, smoky gaslight made it difficult to see faces clearly. Charles the Third didn't seem to be among them—

"And who might you be, darlin'?"

A young man with a shaggy thatch of red hair had come up beside her, a foaming mug in one hand. He'd drained several before this one, from the look of him and his gold-toothed leer. She ignored him after a quick glance, once more searching the room with her eyes.

"How's for company and a glass of lager? Or a wee drop of the crayture?"

Yes, Charles was here! When the Tipperary Bull song ended, from behind the bunched group a spritely and somewhat squawky fiddling commenced—an Irish jig that spurred three of the men into a foot-stomping dance. Charles the Third in his velvet-collared coat was then visible at the far wall, wielding bow and fiddle in an enthusiastic fashion.

Sabina started in his direction. The brash young man said something else and petted her arm; she shook him off, threaded her way across the room past the ogling eyes. Charles was intent on his fiddling; he didn't see her until she was within a few paces of him. His eyes rounded in surprise and he scraped a single false note before recovering and continuing to play until the jig was finished. One of the revelers said something to him, perhaps urging another tune, but Charles shook his head and sidled away along the wall to a table occupied by a ferret-faced individual in a linen cap. An empty chair, the blackthorn stick and empty fiddle case propped against it, and a headless mug of beer indicated this was where he'd been sitting.

He remained upright behind the chair as Sabina approached. His expression was guarded; it was plain that he was not happy to see her, but she detected neither guilt nor guile in his piercing gaze. The group at the bar began another song, this one with ribald lyrics—the singing loud enough so that she had to raise her voice when she spoke.

"So here you are, Uncle Seamus," she said, stressing the word "uncle."

The ferret-faced man glanced up at her, but in a uninterested, bleary-eyed fashion before returning his attention to a large glass of whiskey. He and Charles the Third were evidently nothing more than random tablemates in the crowded room.

"This is no place for you, my lass," Charles said sternly. His affected Irish brogue was almost as thick as that of the clerk at the Dubliner Hotel. "Why have you come?"

"It's urgent that we speak privately, Uncle. Will you please come outside with me?"

He glanced toward the group of singers, his reluctance apparent. But he didn't argue. "As you wish," he said, and proceeded to case his fiddle and bow, tuck the case under his arm. The rounded knob on the blackthorn stick, Sabina noted when he caught it up, bore no telltale signs of blood or damage.

Once outside on the crowded boardwalk, Charles steered

her into the doorway of a closed barbershop. "Explain your-self, Mrs. Carpenter," he said in peevish, now British-accented tones. "Your presence at the pub not only interrupted my ob-servations but placed my mission in Tar Flat in jeopardy. What is of such urgency?"

"Roland Fairchild. The Baldwin Hotel."

His only reaction was one of annoyance. "Yes, yes, I went to see the fellow this morning, as I promised you I would."

"What happened?"

"I made it quite clear to him that my name is Holmes, not Fairchild, that I am in no way related to him, that I have never been in the city of Chicago, and that I have no intention of going there with him or anyone else."

"And then?"

"And then I left him and his rather shrewish wife and re-turned to the Dubliner Hotel."

"Mr. Fairchild was all right when you left?"

"Of course he was. Annoyingly insistent and in something of a temper, but then so was I. I do not take kindly to being in-sulted."

"Did you strike him? With your hands or your stick?"

"Strike him? My dear Mrs. Carpenter, what gave you such a notion?"

"Roland Fairchild is dead," Sabina said. "Brutally blud-geoned to death. Mrs. Fairchild claims you struck the fatal blows with your stick in a sudden frenzy."

He stared at her with his mouth slightly agape. "A foul lie! I have never committed a frenzied act in my life. Nor even a rash one. I am always in perfect control of myself, no matter what the circumstances. As you well know, I am sworn to uphold the law, not to break it."

His shock, indignation, and moral outrage all seemed genuine; she would have sworn he wasn't lying, at least not deliberately. Was it possible the act had been so damaging to his already unbalanced mind that he'd blocked it out completely? Possible, yes, but—

"How did you learn of this outrage, pray tell?"

Sabina told him of her police summons and the words that had been exchanged in the Fairchilds' hotel room.

"I am most grateful to you for not revealing my present whereabouts to the police detectives. You must believe, then, that I am innocent of these monstrous charges."

"I do now, yes."

"Mrs. Fairchild, therefore, is either delusional or she herself is a murderess of the most vicious, calculating, and brazen variety."

Sabina had had the same thought. Octavia Fairchild possessed both the temperament and the physical strength to have battered her husband to death in cold blood—likely with his own walking stick, which had then been hidden before the police arrived. Her motive: a combination of hatred and greed. With Roland Fairchild dead and Charles the Third incarcerated in an institution for the criminally insane, she stood to inherit the entire Fairchild estate as Roland's next of kin.

"It would seem to be the latter."

"Indubitably." Charles's eyes, turned toward Sabina, glowed as if they had been set afire. "So the black widow has ensnared Sherlock Holmes in her web of deceit and made a hunted man of him, has she? The web must therefore be quickly broken, our positions reversed, and the truth will out."

"How?"

"That is yet to be determined. Come, let us walk while I cogitate."

They had gone half a block when Charles muttered, "I dislike playing the fiddle, though I must say I am rather adept at it. I much prefer the violin. Mendelssohn's 'Songs Without Words,' the 'Barcarolle' from Offenbach's *Tales of Hoffman*. Do you know that I have a genuine Stradivarius in my London flat? I acquired it from a broker in Tottenham Court Road for a mere fifty-five shillings."

The skewed way in which Charles the Third's mind worked was a constant source of amazement to Sabina. "What does any of that have to do with—"

"Cogitation takes many forms, ofttimes requiring digression in order to bring fruition." Which sounded like gibberish to Sabina, but she made no comment. They proceeded to the end of the block in silence. Then Charles halted abruptly and demanded, "Were you permitted to view Mr. Fairchild's corpse?"

"No. It was just being taken away when I arrived at the hotel."

"Did the police reveal to you the number of times the victim was coshed?"

"They did. His skull was crushed in four places. Mrs. Fairchild claims she was also struck a glancing blow when she began screaming."

"Did she, now. Were there any marks upon her person to corroborate her claim?"

"Only a small gash on her cheek."

"How small?"

"Two inches or so, below the left cheekbone."

"Was her clothing torn or bloodstained?"

"The dressing gown she wore was unblemished. She must have changed and then hidden her bloodstained clothing along with the weapon she used. The police had little enough reason to search the rooms, given her testimony."

Charles the Third ruminated in silence for another quarter of a block. Then, his eyes burning even brighter, he gave a sharp nod, tapped his blackthorn smartly on the boardwalk, and said, "The strategy is now clear. You and I must once more work together in consort, daringly this time."

"How do you propose we do that?"

"Elementary, dear lady. Our first and most important course of action is a visit to the one place the authorities will never expect to find me."

"And that is?"

"The city morgue."

20

QUINCANNON

The eight A.M. ferry for Sausalito left on schedule, but the SF&NP train for Los Alegres was twenty minutes late. Typical railroad inefficiency, though the delay was minimal enough.

On the train, Quincannon shared a seat with an undersized drummer of drug sundries. ("Everything from female complaint medicine to prophylactics," the little man said confidentially, tapping his sample case.) The drummer, as gregarious as most of his breed, had spent twenty years traveling the counties north of San Francisco; when he learned that his seatmate knew relatively little about the Los Alegres area, he offered a font of local anecdotes and historical detail. Quincannon paid attention to some of it, asking questions now and then, because having a useful amount of information about an unfamiliar place was always beneficial.

There were six hatcheries in Los Alegres, of which the Pioneer was the second largest. Dozens of small chicken farms thrived in the outlying areas; if the one belonging to a widow named Ella was one of them, the drummer had no knowledge of it. The town had better than fifty saloons—

"drinking hells," the salesman called them, adding unnecessarily that he himself was a temperance man—and the nearby hills were "riddled with bootlegging stills." Nonetheless, he admitted, the town was "mostly a respectable place. Haven't been but half a dozen murders and one hanging since it was incorporated."

A good horse could be rented at Gilford's Livery on Main Street above Steamer Basin. And if Quincannon was interested in "letting his hair down some," why, there was a spot out near a place called the Haystacks that was run by a right friendly woman named Belle . . .

The time passed swiftly enough, the drummer's droning voice and the rhythmic clacking of steel on steel putting Quincannon into a half doze. But he was on his feet as soon as the engineer whistled down for the Los Alegres station, interrupting one of the salesman's monologues with a hasty word of parting. When the locomotive hissed to a stop he was the first passenger off the cars.

The day was cold and overcast here, as it had been in the city. Green hills stretched out to the east, beyond miles of open farmland. To the west he could see the brown line of the estuary, its banks lined with feed and grain mills, and the town proper beyond.

He boarded a horse-drawn cable car that took him across the estuary to Main Street. It was a four-block walk to the Pioneer Hatchery, a winged brick building on a corner lot. From the clerk he spoke to he learned that one of their former suppliers of eggs were the Draycotts, Samuel and Ella, whose farm was several miles east. Former? Samuel had died some three months before and the farm had fallen on hard times; that was all the clerk would say. Never having been there, he was unable to provide adequate directions.

Quincannon considered a visit to Lincoln Evans, the town constable, and decided it was premature. Instead he found his way to Gilford's Livery, opposite a city park. This was the right choice, for not only did the hostler have a good horse for hire—a lean and sturdy claybank—but he knew the Draycotts and was willing to share his knowledge without prying into Quincannon's reasons for asking.

"Sam and me were friends," he said. "I used to go out to his place all the time to play euchre. Fine man, Sam. Shocked me when I heard he died. Caught the grippe and it turned into pneumonia just about overnight."

"How has Mrs. Draycott been bearing up?"

"Better than you'd expect. First all the troubles they had with the farm, then Sam up and dying so sudden. Plenty of women would've took to their beds. But Miz Draycott, she's a strong one."

"What sort of troubles?"

"Whole string of 'em. Chicken disease wiped out more than a hundred of their laying hens. Been real dry around here for a year now, and they had a poor alfalfa crop. Then the barn caught fire and burned down. Some folks been saying the place is jinxed, probably why it hasn't been sold by now, but I don't hold with that kind of talk."

"The property is for sale, then?"

"Ever since Sam died. More than fair price, too."

Quincannon said, "I'm looking for a man named Corby, Elias Corby, who may be interested in buying it. A bookkeeper for Golden State Steam Beer in San Francisco. Would you happen to know him?"

"Corby, Corby. No, the name don't ring any bells."

Quincannon described him, but the description rang no bells for Gilford, either. But then he said, "San Francisco, you say? Ella Draycott's brother lives down there, now I think of it. Teamster, makes his living driving a beer wagon. Mebbe that's how this Corby fella heard about the Draycott farm being for sale."

Likely it was. "Is Mrs. Draycott still living at the farm?"

"Sure is. Wouldn't hear of moving into town. Said she didn't want to put nobody out."

"Alone, or is there a hired hand to help her with the chores?

"No, sir, just her now. Sam had to let their last hired man go two months before he died."

"Well, I believe I'll pay a call on the widow. How do I get to her farm, Mr. Gilford?"

"It's about four mile out Oak Creek Road," the hostler said. "Easy enough to find." He went on to give directions to Oak Creek Road, and described a landmark that would identify the wagon trail leading in to the Draycott property.

Quincannon paid in advance for the claybank, left his grip in the hostler's care, and rode out of town to the northeast, following Gilford's directions. The claybank was spirited and wanted to run; Quincannon held him down for a while, because it had been some time since he'd sat a saddle and the one Gilford had rented him was old, worn, and of an unfamiliar design. But he was used to it by the time he reached the cutoff for Oak Creek Road and he gave the horse his head, letting him canter for a mile or so before hauling him down again.

The road wound through rich farmland, much too fallow and dry-looking for this time of year. The creek paralleling the road was little more than half full. San Francisco had had only a small share of rain this winter, likewise this region—not nearly enough to put an end to the long dry spell.

A sharp wind made the ride a cold one, even bundled as he was in his chesterfield, his hands gloved, a scarf tied chin-high around his neck. A farm wagon drawn by two horses and piled high with crates of eggs clattered by; otherwise the road was deserted. The only people he saw aside from the wagon driver were men working here and there in the fields. He passed two poultry ranches, identifiable as such by rows of long, low, shedlike henhouses. The wind carried the faintly audible clucking of innumerable chickens.

The landmark the hostler had told him about—a lightning-struck live oak—appeared ahead. Quincannon slowed the claybank. The rutted wagon trail was visible beyond the tree, angling away across a short meadow; but a low, grassy hill hid the farm from the road. That suited him. He wanted a look at the place from a safe distance before he went near it, and that hill might do. There was cover along its brow; more live oaks, manzanita, and some bare rocks jutting up through the green and brown grass.

He turned onto the trail, but left it after a short distance and walked the horse across the meadow and up along the backbone of the hill. Near the crown he dismounted, ground-reined the animal, then moved up among the rocks to where he could see what lay on the far side.

The farm was there, tucked into a little hollow, flanked on two sides by alfalfa fields. From where he stood, the farm buildings were better than three hundred yards away. He could see a flock of brown and white hens pecking the ground behind chicken-wire fencing alongside one of four henhouses, a couple of horses inside a pole corral with a lean-to shelter at the near end. There was no sign of human habitation, but a buckboard was visible under the lean-to, and someone was inside the farmhouse. A thin column of chimney smoke spiraled up into the gray sky.

The property did in fact have a gone-to-seed look. The small farmhouse and chicken coops were in need of whitewash; the remains of the burned-out barn sat off to one side, all but a single wall collapsed into rubble and that one leaning like a collection of fire-blackened bones; the small windmill had lost two of its blades; the unplowed fields showed their neglect. Only a vegetable garden alongside the house appeared, at least from a distance, to have been tended to by the widow Draycott.

A place that was dying, that would be as dead as Samuel Draycott in less than a year if someone didn't take it in hand. There was something sad and lonesome about it—a blighted, tragic place. The only sounds that reached Quincannon's ears were the squawking of the chickens and the irregular, rhythmic scree of the windmill's remaining blades turning in the wind. Like the beat of a bad heart. Like the beginnings of a death rattle.

Why was Elias Corby interested in buying it? Quincannon wondered. The bookkeeper hadn't struck him as the type who secretly yearned to be a farmer, or would be willing to indulge in the sort of hard physical labor it would take to make this place productive again. Surely he'd seen it before, met its sur-viving owner . . . Ah, that was the answer. It wasn't the farm he coveted so much as it was the widow Draycott. Obsessive designs on her as well as her land was the likely impetus for his transformation from reasonably honest bookkeeper into thief and murderer.

Quincannon continued to watch the farmhouse, consider-ing his options. If his quarry had arranged to stay there, he couldn't very well ride in openly; Corby would have armed himself, and a man who had already killed twice wouldn't hes-itate to make an ambush try for number three in order to save himself. The safest course of action, then, was to make a co-vert approach and utilize the element of surprise. Safe, that was, unless Corby was not holed up here and the widow her-self was armed—a likelihood for a woman living alone—and had keen eyes and no qualms about shooting a trespassing stranger.

He studied the surrounding terrain. The hill he was on spread out to the south, sloping down gradually to a shallow gully where the creek flowed. The gully ran along two hundred yards or so to the rear of the farm buildings, through humped-up meadowland and a stand of willows. To the west, beyond the untilled alfalfa fields, the land rose again into a series of short, rolling hillocks. There was no cover in that direction, none anywhere within a fifty-yard radius of the buildings. The only reasonably safe way to make his approach was on a diag-onal from the rear, from where this hill leveled out at the gully—and at that, it meant crossing those two hundred yards of open ground to either the remains of the barn or the nearest of the chicken coops.

The cold wind gusted, causing the screech of the ungreased windmill blades to rise in volume. Quincannon's jaw clenched; that noise, constant on windy days, would fray a man's nerves raw. Just a few minutes of it had put an extra twist of tension between his shoulder blades.

He backed down below the crown of the hill and went laterally along its backbone, descending toward the gully. The windmill shrieks weren't as loud here, mercifully. When he reached the gully he followed its westward progress to where a lone willow drooped its branches down over the bank. He stopped there because he could see the farm buildings again. Still no sign of anyone out and about.

Quincannon opened his coat to allow free access to his holstered Navy Colt, then followed the gully a ways farther before cutting away from it across the rocky meadow, running with his body bent low. He kept his eyes lifted as he ran, his gaze steady on the farmhouse; a shaft of sunlight shining through a rift in the cloud cover glinted off the glass in its rear windows, so if there was movement behind them he couldn't detect it. The back door remained closed, the farmyard empty.

The first of the henhouses was the closest structure; he veered toward it, putting the coop between himself and the house. When he reached its back wall he eased along it and around the far side, along the chicken-wire fencing in front. Some of the hens scratching inside the yard set up a minor ruckus, but he judged it wasn't enough to alert whoever was inside the house. He continued at an angle through the vegetable patch, still watching the house's backside. He could see into the windows now, past faded muslin curtains. No one was there to look back at him.

Dry cornstalks crunched under his feet; he sidestepped onto clear ground, slowing. The back stoop was straight ahead, but he bypassed it, went to the near corner and along the side wall. Toward the front was another window, its sash raised a few inches. He stopped alongside it and half squatted so that his ear was on a level with the opening.

The murmur of voices came from inside, a man's and a woman's, but they were in another room and he could only make out a few of the words—not enough so that there was any sense to them, or to tell if the man's was familiar. He eased his head up and around for a quick look through the glass. The room, a sparsely furnished front parlor, was empty. Until he was certain of the man's identity, he was loath to take the risk of entering. He stayed where he was, listening, watching, waiting.

Better than five minutes passed. The voices halted briefly, grew in volume when they began again. A few moments later, the woman came into the parlor through a rear doorway— tallish, spare, wearing a calico traveling dress and bonnet. Behind her was the man, and as soon as Quincannon had a clear look at him, his lips peeled back into a dragon's grin.

Elias Corby, no mistake.

21

QUINCANNON

Corby, dressed in farm clothing, was saying to the woman, ". . . and you can wait here, Ella, while I hitch up the buckboard." Without waiting for an answer, he strode quickly to the front door.

Quincannon was upright and moving by then, his fingers tight around the butt of his Navy Colt. He heard the door slam shut, then Corby clumping down off the porch. When he reached the corner of the porch and stepped around it, the little man was on his way across the yard toward the lean-to at the corral's near end. He wore no sidearm and his hands were free, but that did not have to mean he was unarmed. Quincannon let him get another ten paces away from the house, so that he was in the middle of the yard with nothing around him for cover and no easy avenue of escape. Then he stepped out around the porch with the revolver up and thumbed to cock.

"Elias Corby!"

Corby jerked to a halt, spun on his heels. His hands came up the way a prizefighter's will, held still in that position. He blinked, staring; disbelief slackened his jaw when he recognized Quincannon. His eyes goggled with the onset of panic.

"Stand fast! Hands up over your head!"

Corby did the opposite: he spun again and ran.

The movement was so sudden that Quincannon hesitated a second or two before shouting, "Stop, Corby, or take a bullet!" But the blasted fool kept on running, heading on a line for the corral.

Quincannon could have fired at him, aiming low for the legs, but he had a strong aversion to shooting any man from behind. Even if he'd felt differently, firing a shot to bring Corby down would not have been necessary. The little man tripped in his haste and fell sprawling, hurting himself enough in the process so that he was unable to haul himself upright. Quincannon, running, saw him roll the last couple of yards to the corral fence, then under the bottom rail into the corral. The two farm horses were plunging in there, frightened by the commotion. Corby avoided them, scrambling crabwise into the lean-to.

Again Quincannon held his fire. Behind him he could hear the widow Draycott screaming, but he didn't turn his head. For a couple of seconds he lost sight of Corby in the shadows alongside the buckboard; he was almost to the fence when the little bookkeeper reappeared, upright now in an awkward stance.

In his hands was a double-barreled shotgun.

An instant before he cut loose with the first barrel, Quincannon threw himself sideways to the hard ground. The load of buckshot blew away part of one fence rail and peppered the yard harmlessly. Still on his belly, Quincannon steadied the Navy and fired twice. Both reports were lost in a second boom from the shotgun, but one of his bullets had struck Corby in the upper body, the impact jerking the shotgun's long barrel skyward so that the pellets came hailing down forty yards from where he lay.

Corby collapsed to his knees, let go of the shotgun, and toppled over on his back. The horses were half mad with terror now, neighing and snorting and pawing the ground, but they shied away from Corby's twitching form. As Quincannon scrambled to his feet, he saw Ella Draycott in a rigid stance halfway across the yard behind him. Screaming words now in a shrill voice, "You killed him! Murderer, murderer!"

That he is, madam. Twice a murderer.

He went ahead to the fence, leaned against it for a few seconds to steady himself before he climbed through. Corby lay still on the straw- and manure-spattered earth, the shotgun near one outflung arm, his thin, long-nosed features twisted into a grimace of pain. There was a spreading stain of blood on the front of his linsey-woolsey shirt, but the bullet wound was above the left nipple and the slug seemed not to have severed a major artery. Not only still alive, but apparently in no imminent danger of succumbing to his wound.

Quincannon picked up the shotgun and tossed it aside, even though it was no longer a threat. Then he bent and ran his free hand over Corby's clothing to satisfy himself that the felon carried no hideout weapon. Only then did he holster his Navy. Corby stared up at him with pain-dulled eyes that had lost none of their disbelief.

"How . . . damn you, how did you find me?"

"With less effort than you might suppose. It was blind luck you got away from me in the city, and no man escapes John Quincannon twice, no matter where he goes to hide."

The widow Draycott was no longer shrieking. She approached warily, her hand fisted at her mouth, and stopped near the fence to peer in at Corby. "Elias?" she said.

Quincannon said, "Not dead, Mrs. Draycott, as you can plainly see."

"Elias?" she said again, but Corby turned his head away and closed his eyes. Her gaze shifted to Quincannon. "How do you know my name? Who are you?"

"John Quincannon. Detective from San Francisco."

"Detective? But . . . I don't . . . Why did you shoot Elias?"

"My investigations led me to believe he could be found here and I came to take him into custody. He is wanted for theft and two murders in San Francisco."

Shock caused her to gasp, then to wag her head brokenly. "Elias Corby, a murderer? It can't be. He . . . he and I . . ."

"What reason did he give you for coming here and asking to stay?"

"He . . . he said he'd come into some funds, that he wanted to use it to fix up the place . . . that he wanted us to be . . . Oh, my Lord!"

"Did he give you any money?"

"Five hundred dollars. Will I not be able to keep it?"

Quincannon flicked a glance around the rundown farm-yard, then returned it to the woman who now looked as though she might burst into tears. He said, "You can keep it as far as I'm concerned, though I wouldn't mention it to Constable Evans in Los Alegres."

"No. Oh, no, I won't."

"Corby's wound needs tending to before I take him to jail.

Sulfa powder, bandages. Laudanum, if you have it. Blankets, too."

"No laudanum, but the rest, yes . . . yes . . ." She started away, but he called her back.

"Did Corby bring any luggage with him?"

"Only a small grip."

"Fetch that, too."

She nodded and hurried off with her calico skirts lifted.

Quincannon knelt beside Corby. "You're finished now, man, so you might as well make a full confession. Xavier Jones already has," he added, stretching the truth some.

"Go to hell," Corby said, his eyes still closed.

"You'll roast there long before me, I'll wager. But none too soon if you're cooperative. The quicker you come clean, the better your chances of cheating the hangman."

"Go to hell."

Quincannon stretched the truth a little farther by saying, "You and Caleb Lansing were hired to steal the steam beer recipe, on orders from Cyrus Drinkwater. Jones claims you knew Drinkwater was behind the scheme from the start."

"He's . . . a goddamn liar."

"We both know he isn't. Admit it, Corby, and you and Jones won't be the only two to face a judge and jury."

"I . . . I . . ." The rest of what Corby had been trying to say was lost in a spasm of coughing. His face, contorted with pain, had taken on a grayish cast. When the coughing ceased, his body sagged and was still.

Just as well that he'd lapsed into unconsciousness, for Ella Draycott was returning with an armful of medical supplies and heavy wool blankets and a small black valise. Quincannon un-buttoned Corby's shirt to expose the bloody bullet wound. She didn't flinch at the sight of it; farm women were a hardy lot, used to the sight of blood and torn flesh. Without looking at Quincannon, she knelt and began a makeshift dressing of the wound with sulfa powder, gauze, and adhesive tape.

While she was doing that, he opened the grip. It contained a few items of cheap clothing that Corby must have bought be-fore leaving San Francisco, and a purse containing a wad of greenbacks and gold eagles. Quincannon gave the bills and coins a quick count. More than five thousand dollars—Corby's share of the payoff for the stolen formula, which he'd gathered wherever it had been secreted, plus what he'd pilfered from Caleb Lansing's rooms. Leaving the money where it was, Quincannon closed the grip and carried it with him into the lean-to where he hitched up the buckboard. The horses were over their fright and gave him no trouble.

The widow had finished her ministrations by the time he brought the wagon out to where Corby lay breathing ster-torously, still unconscious. That made the task of lifting the man a simple one. The widow spread out a blanket on the wagon bed, and when Quincannon laid his burden atop it, she covered Corby with a second blanket.

"It's a rough ride to town," she said then. "I'd best go with you."

"As you please, Mrs. Draycott. I have a rented horse pick-eted nearby; we'll have to collect him on the way, but it shouldn't take long."

She had nothing to say to that. She waited until Quincan-non had stepped up to the seat and picked up the reins, then climbed into the wagon bed and sat in stoic silence with her back against the sideboard and Corby's head pillowed in her lap.

Constable Lincoln Evans was a middle-aged gent with a competent, no-nonsense manner. He listened without interruption to Quincannon's account of what had taken place on the Draycott farm, his acceptance of it bolstered by mention of Mr. Boggs's name and Quincannon's former association with the Secret Service chief. Quincannon had no qualms about turning the large amount of cash in Corby's grip over to the lawman for safekeeping; Boggs had proclaimed him honest and there could be no higher recommendation.

Evans sent his deputy to fetch a doctor, spoke soothingly to a taciturn Ella Draycott, and helped Quincannon carry the wounded man inside and onto a cot in one of three cells. Corby had regained consciousness on the ride in, but if he'd had anything to say, it was in an undertone to the widow. In his weakened condition, he'd posed no threat of another escape.

He was still conscious after the doctor had come and gone, having confirmed that the bullet wound was not life-threatening. Quincannon, with Constable Evans present, then made another fruitless effort to convince the prisoner to confess and implicate Cyrus Drinkwater. All his blandishments were met with stony silence. Mayhap the San Francisco police, once Corby was in their custody, would be able to coerce a confession out of him. But that would not be for some time, until he was healthy enough to be transported to the city; until then

Evans agreed to keep him locked up here on a charge of attempted murder.

A confession from Corby would have made it easier to bring about Drinkwater's arrest and a conspiracy charge against him. Without it, Xavier Jones was the only man who could directly implicate his boss. Would he, if pressed hard enough? Perhaps, but his fear of the cutthroat businessman's power and of potential reprisal might be as great as Corby's.

Quincannon's most sensible option upon his return, therefore, was to take the facts he'd gathered and his suspicions to James Willard and thence to the police. With Willard's support, he ought to be able to convince Kleinhoffer and his superiors at the Hall of Justice of the guilt of Corby and Jones. Drinkwater, with his powerful political connections, might get off scot-free even if he were compromised by one or both of his hirelings—a galling thought. If that happened, the onus would be on the nabbers for failing to build a solid case against him, not on John Frederick Quincannon.

But before he went to either his client or the police, there was one more task to be accomplished—the most important of all, if he were to justify his fee and mark this case closed.

He must find a way to recover the stolen steam beer formula and return it James Willard himself, personally.

22

Charles the Third had been completely serious about a visit to the city morgue. In his usual secretive fashion he kept his specific intentions to himself, saying only "that is where the evidence lies." Even when he explained his plan to gain access to the body of Roland Fairchild, which required her assistance, Sabina didn't try to talk him out of it. Nor, after some reflection, did she refuse to take part in the scheme, despite the fact that it was bold, dangerous, and in keeping with its creator, more than a little mad. She thought she knew what he expected to find, and if he did, those findings would help prove that not he but Octavia Fairchild had slain her husband.

Stephen would have counseled her against taking part in the scheme. So would John, and so did her professional instincts. If she and Charles were caught, it would mean arrest for aiding and abetting a fugitive and irreparable harm to her reputation and that of Carpenter and Quincannon, Professional Detective Services; Homer Keeps, for one, would vilify her in print. Yet in spite of Charles's often infuriating habits and methods, she had grown almost fond of him. And she was convinced, now, that he was incapable of an act of wanton violence. In all good conscience, she simply could not abandon an innocent man to the life of a fugitive or the none-too-tender mercies of the law if he were caught.

His plan for gaining access to Roland Fairchild's remains was clever enough; if they were careful and luck were with them, it might well succeed. After all, as Charles had stated, the morgue, which was in a basement adjunct to the Hall of Justice, was the last place the police would expect to find him. Another of his disguises would make recognition all but impossible, and still another for Sabina, he said, would camouflage her identity as well.

"What sort of disguise do you expect me to wear?" she asked.

"One perfect for the occasion, as you'll see."

"Washerwoman, prostitute?"

"Nothing so plebeian. Quite suitable, I assure you."

"Tell me, Charles—"

"Kindly do not refer to me by that name," he said, bristling. "How many times must I insist that the Fairchild family was wrong, quite wrong, in their claim of my lineage. I am a British subject, *not* an American."

"I'm sorry." Trying to convince him to admit that he was not S. Holmes, Esquire, was hopeless. "Tell me, Sherlock . . . I may call you Sherlock?"

"You may."

"Where do you obtain so many different disguises? Do you have a storehouse of them hidden somewhere?"

"That, dear lady," he said with one of his enigmatic smiles, "is a secret I do not wish to divulge."

The morgue—Sabina had been there once previously—was closed to visitors on Sunday evenings. Even if it hadn't been, time was needed, Charles said, to make preparations—presumably the procuring of their disguises. Therefore they decided, or rather he decided, that early Monday morning shortly after opening was the time to carry out their objective. He would arrive at her flat at eight A.M., and from there they would travel together the short distance to the Hall of Justice at Portsmouth Square.

She was somewhat reluctant to let him out of her sight for such a long period of time, but she couldn't very well spend the night with him even if he were to permit it, which he wouldn't. She left him in Tar Flat and returned home. Throughout the long evening, she kept wondering if she hadn't been as daft as he was to agree to his plan, and she slept poorly. But on Monday morning, her belief in his innocence remained steadfast and she was ready if not eager to proceed with it.

There was a separate entrance to the morgue on a side street off Kearney, but to get to it required running a gantlet of arriving and departing uniformed officers and police vehicles. An uneventful running, as it turned out; no one paid any attention to Sabina and Charles the Third. He was dressed in sedate gentleman's clothing, carrying a furled umbrella instead of his usual blackthorn stick, sporting a bushy theatrical beard that covered most of his lean features, and walking with a slight but noticeable limp. She wore the disguise he'd brought for her, which thank heaven was more appropriate than she'd worried it would be—a plain black dress, a black veil, and a plain black hat over a wig of dark red curls. Even John or Callie would have had to look closely to recognize her.

The morgue was a dank, gloomy place rife with unpleasant odors. Plans were in the offing to build, in addition to a new Hall of Justice on the present site, a separate morgue building— one that would contain several tiled rooms including one for postmortem examinations, a cold-storage plant for the keeping of bodies and pathological specimens, and a viewing room. The coroner's office would be on the second floor, made large enough so that inquests could be held in it, and there would also be facilities for the deliberation of coroner's juries. But this expansion and restructuring was a minimum of two years off. The present outmoded facilities were cramped and inadequate, the walls of brick and decaying wooden panels.

The attendant who this morning presided over the cold room in which cadavers were kept and necropsies performed was a white-maned, pinch-faced individual nearing the age of retirement. He was ensconced in an anteroom cubicle, seated at a desk behind a low counter and reading the *Morning Call,* when Sabina and Charles the Third entered. The anteroom, she was relieved to note, was otherwise empty and no sounds came from behind the closed door to the cold room.

The attendant lowered his newspaper and peered at them with an expression of bored civility. Sabina's mourning outfit seemed not to affect him in the slightest. Too many years spent dwelling in the shadow of death, she thought.

"Yes?" he said, stifling a yawn. "Something I can do for you folks?"

"I am Mrs. Roland W. Fairchild," Sabina said through the veil. She put a slight grieving throb into her voice; weeping would have overdone it. "I should like to view my husband's remains."

"Fairchild. Fairchild. Gent who was . . . who died at the Baldwin Hotel yesterday?"

"Yes."

"My condolences." A by-rote remark with no feeling behind it.

"Thank you."

"But I don't know as I should allow it. Coroner might not approve."

"Why should he disapprove of a widow viewing her poor husband's mortal remains one last time?"

"Last time?"

"Before I arrange for shipment to his final resting place in Chicago."

"View him there before he's buried, can't you?"

"No. He's to be cremated."

This brought a censorious frown to the attendant's pinched face. "Don't approve of burning up the dead. Downright unchristian, if you ask me."

"It was the deceased's wishes," Charles the Third said, abandoning his faux British accent in favor of an American one that betrayed his Midwestern roots. "Now kindly be so good as to honor Mrs. Fairchild's request. She is under a severe strain, as you can well imagine."

"You also a relative of the deceased?"

"No. I am John Mycroft, Mrs. Fairchild's attorney. I, too, wish to view the remains."

"That so? Why?"

"I have just told you, my good man. I am Mrs. Fairchild's

attorney, engaged by her only this morning to safeguard her interests. I have not yet had an opportunity to observe the, ah, damage that was done to my client's husband. I assume that an autopsy has yet to be performed, not that one would be necessary under the circumstances."

"There'll be one, like as not, but I don't know when." The attendant scratched his white mane, then added in an aggrieved tone, "Nobody tells me nothing."

Charles said, "I suggest a regular application of one-quarter cup apple cider vinegar mixed with water."

"Eh?"

"There is no more effective cure for dandruff."

The attendant gaped at him. "How'd you know I had dandruff? Can't see it on my coat from where you're standing."

"But I can. I could also tell by the manner in which you scratched your scalp. I have keen vision and I am a trained observer of trifles—"

Sabina prodded Charles's shin with the toe of her shoe, none too gently. "May we view my husband's remains now, sir?"

"Apple cider vinegar, eh? Never thought of that. I'll sure give it a try." The attendant produced a ledger and slid it onto the counter. "Have to sign your names before I can let you inside."

Sabina signed first, then Charles with a Spencerian flourish. The attendant stood after removing the book, plucked a ring of keys off a wall peg, and came out to unlock the door to the cold room. He led them inside, saying, "Don't want to stay in here too long, folks. Too cold, might catch your death." An old, unfunny, and rather offensive joke; he barely managed to suppress a chuckle at his half wit.

The cadavers were kept inside wooden drawers that opened

out from the wall on rollers. The attendant slid one open, drew the sheet back to reveal the corpse of Roland Fairchild. Sabina winced in spite of herself when she saw the wounds that had crushed her former client's skull; they had obviously been struck with considerable force.

Protocol demanded that the attendant remain in the room with them, so Sabina's task now was to distract him while Charles the Third examined the body. After a few seconds, she moved away to stand to one side and somewhat behind him, so that when she said, "Do you have many cadavers here at present?" he had to turn toward her to answer the inane question.

"Nine. Two homicides, two drownings, four natural causes."

"Is that an unusually large number?"

"Nope. Had near twenty once, a while back, most of 'em heathen Chinee killed in a tong war."

Charles had produced a large magnifying glass and was peering at each of the head wounds. She heard him murmur, "Plain as a pikestaff," but if the attendant also heard, he gave no indication of it.

She said, "But there are only twelve drawers. What was done to keep the rest?"

"Laid out on the floor. Heathen Chinee, like I said, so it didn't matter none."

Now Charles drew the sheet down to the corpse's waist, lifted the left hand, and squinted at it briefly through his glass. Then he lowered it and picked up the right hand to study. "Ah! Just as I expected," he said, and this time the attendant heard him.

"Here now, mister. What're you doing there?"

"Merely examining the deceased."

"With a glass? What for?"

"Thoroughness, my good man. I am nothing if not thorough."

"You ain't supposed to touch the bodies."

"My apologies, sir. I'm afraid I became carried away."

"Some folks got no respect for rules and regulations," the attendant muttered. He moved over to the drawer, drew the sheet back up over the corpse's face, then slid the drawer back into the wall. "I think you folks better leave now."

"Indeed. With all dispatch."

They had just stepped out of the cold room when the anteroom door opened and a uniformed policeman entered—a sergeant according to his stripes. Sabina held her breath, but he did nothing more than remove his cap in deference to her apparent bereavement, and barely glanced at Charles the Third. They made their exit without incident.

As they stepped outside Sabina murmured, "Do you suppose the attendant will say anything about your close examination of the corpse?"

"We needn't worry about that. To his sparsely populated brain attic, it was merely a minor breach."

Neither of them spoke again as they passed out of the shadow of the Hall of Justice and safely across Portsmouth Square. The temperature in the morgue's cold room mingled with that of the overcast, windy morning had chilled Sabina to the bone. Charles the Third must have felt it, too; he offered no objection when she took his arm and steered him into the warmth of a small and mostly empty café.

Over cups of steaming liquid, coffee for her, English tea for

Charles, she said, "I take it you found what you were looking for in your examination."

"Quite." His British accent was back in place. "Evidence that will help to exonerate me and place the burden of guilt where it belongs, on the Fairchild woman. You know the nature of the evidence, of course?"

"Yes."

"I was sure you did. Your brain attic is quite in order, as always."

Sabina ignored that remark. She'd heard more than enough of the brain attic metaphor to last her the rest of her days. "But we both know it's not enough to convince Lieutenant McGinn."

"Not by itself, no."

"There may not be any more proof. Mrs. Fairchild has had ample time to see to that."

"Has she?" Charles sipped his tea. "Perhaps not."

"She's far too cunning not to dispose of anything that might incriminate her, and the morgue evidence is inconclusive. Without something more, your innocence and her guilt can't be proven beyond a reasonable doubt."

"Ah, but it can. By means of careful arrangement."

"Arrangement? Of what?"

"A damning confession delivered in front of witnesses, which the evidence will then conclusively support."

Sabina looked at him askance. "A coldhearted, clever murderess such as Octavia Fairchild would never willingly confess, especially not in front of witnesses."

"Witnesses need only be ear, not eye. And 'willingly' is a relative term."

"Surely you're not thinking of using force—"

"My dear Mrs. Carpenter," Charles said in an offended tone. "Sherlock Holmes never resorts to crude physical tactics. Never!"

"Well, in any case, returning to the Baldwin Hotel to confront her would be a foolish risk."

"Indeed it would." He tapped his temple with a bony forefinger. "No, what is in my brain attic is far more provocative."

Brain attic again. As John would say, faugh!

"Well, then?"

"If Muhammed is unable to go to the mountain, then the mountain must come to Muhammed."

"For heaven's sake, stop speaking in riddles. How do you expect to make her confess?"

"I don't," he said through one of his sly smiles. "That task, dear lady, is to be yours."

23

SABINA

Charles the Third's method of inducing a confession from Octavia Fairchild had merit, though whether or not it would work was problematical. It depended, among other factors, on how well Sabina played her role and how easily the Fairchild woman could be duped and manipulated. But as he pointed out, there was no other logical way to prove his innocence and thus "restore the good name of Sherlock Holmes."

The plan, unlike the one for access to the city morgue, required a considerable amount of preparation on Sabina's part. Her first step, upon leaving the café near Portsmouth Square (minus mourning veil and red wig), was a short trolley ride to the offices of Carpenter and Quincannon, Professional Detective Services. Where Charles was bound he wouldn't tell her, saying only that he would meet her there at the agreed-upon hour. It was her hope that John would be at the agency; despite the amount of explaining necessary to elicit his aid, he was naturally her first choice as the primary witness to her forthcoming playlet with the Fairchild woman. But he wasn't there. Hadn't been there at all since she'd last seen him on

Thursday afternoon, judging by the absence of messages and the vague mustiness that always accumulated when the agency had been untenanted for a couple of days.

At her desk, with the window behind her open to let in fresh air, Sabina composed a carefully worded, cryptic note on the agency's letterhead. Since the time had yet to be determined, she left that space blank for the present.

> *Mrs. Fairchild:*
> *I know that you and not Charles Fairchild the Third murdered your husband. I know your motive for the crime, and I am in possession of proof of your guilt. You would be well advised to present yourself at my office at the above address at   o'clock this afternoon for a private discussion of the matter.*

Sabina signed her name, folded the letterhead, slid it inside a matching envelope, and put the unsealed envelope in her handbag. In the event John should put in an appearance, she then wrote a note to him asking that he wait for her return and placed it on his desk blotter.

Leaving the window open slightly, she locked up again and went downstairs to the offices of Archer and Boone, Searchers of Records and Conveyancers—a firm which specialized in the examination of titles and abstracts in counties throughout the state, and whose services she and John had utilized on more than one occasion. Edward Boone, a spear of a man with an elongated head and the longest, thinnest neck on any human being she'd ever seen (John referred to him privately and amiably as "the giraffe"), was his usual accommodating self: he agreed, once she briefly explained the situation to him, to act as the necessary witness.

A cab delivered Sabina to her rooms, where she changed into her normal business attire, and then took her to the Baldwin Hotel. This was her most important stop. If the plan were to be put into action this afternoon, Octavia Fairchild had still to be in residence there and either present or soon to return. Luck or divine providence, as it turned out, was on Sabina's side. Yes, the desk clerk told her solemnly and warily, Mrs. Fairchild was still registered, though she had been given different accommodations; and yes, she was in her room, though she had left instructions not to be disturbed.

Sabina gave him her card, explaining that her business with Mrs. Fairchild vitally concerned yesterday's tragic events. Would he have one of the bellboys deliver a sealed note to her? Yes, he would. At a lobby writing desk, Sabina filled in the time of 2:00 in the blank space in the note, sealed the envelope, and handed it to the clerk. No, she said, it wouldn't be necessary for her to wait for an answer.

She took another hansom to the agency offices, but before entering she bought a packet of fresh shrimp, a soft pretzel, and a large apple at the market across the street. She hadn't eaten anything except two biscuits all day and her stomach was making rumbling demands. John still hadn't returned. She ate at her desk, then cleaned up some of the clutter in the small closed alcove where records and supplies were kept. The space was small, but sufficient for two persons to stand together with the door drawn to. A walk down the hall to the bathroom facilities, a walk from there downstairs to confirm her arrangements with Edward Boone, and a check of her Remington derringer and placement of it in her slightly open desk drawer used up a few more minutes. The time then was 12:48.

Everything was in place, all the preparations completed. There was nothing to do now but wait. Soon Charles the Third would arrive, then Edward Boone. And then Octavia Fairchild. If Sabina's and Charles's assessment of the woman's character was correct, she would come alone and in a coldly controlled fury.

Charles, predictably enough, wore his Sherlock Holmes outfit of Inverness cape and deerstalker hat; he was even smoking his long, curved meerschaum pipe. When she told him all was in readiness, he said, "Splendid, splendid. I felt certain that it would be," and then made himself comfortable behind John's desk. Sabina hid a smile when she imagined the expression on her partner's face if he were to walk in just then and find his nemesis occupying his chair.

Ten minutes later, at 1:30, Edward Boone appeared. His eyes widened and his Adam's apple twice traveled up and down the long column of his neck when Sabina introduced Charles as Mr. S. Holmes. He said impulsively, "The fellow who claims to be the famous detective, Sherlock Holmes?"

"Claims, my good man? Claims? I *am* Sherlock Holmes."

Edward somewhat bewilderedly appealed to Sabina. "But . . . he's wanted for the murder yesterday at the Baldwin Hotel. Surely you're not harboring a fugitive mental—" He caught himself before finishing the sentence, his Adam's apple bobbing again.

"Mental case, sir?" Charles said stiffly. "Hardly. Mrs. Carpenter evidently failed to explain that I am neither a mental case nor a murderer, but the victim of false accusations and an attempted conspiracy."

"Yes, and I apologize for my omission of those details," Sabina said. The fact was she had deliberately omitted mention of Charles the Third's identities, real and assumed, for fear that Edward would not agree to act as a witness if he knew in advance. "Mr. Holmes is indeed the victim of false accusations and an attempted conspiracy. As we hope to prove when the real criminal arrives shortly."

"And whom would that be?"

"The dead man's wife."

No more information was required to convince Edward; he had been exposed often enough to the exploits of Carpenter and Quincannon, Professional Detective Services, to trust in their judgment. This was fortunate in more ways than one, for there came a sharp rapping on the office door which Sabina had locked after Edward's arrival—Octavia Fairchild, ten minutes early.

Sabina quickly shooed Charles and Edward into the alcove, its door left open a crack so they could hear more easily. Then she admitted their quarry and the game was on.

There were no outward signs of the anger and consternation the Fairchild woman must be feeling. Her face reminded Sabina of an ice sculpture. The blue eyes, fixed and unblinking, were glacial; even the strip of court plaster covering the gash on her cheek seemed frozen in place. She wore an expensive muskrat coat and matching hat, both of which looked to be brand-new and probably were—gifts to herself for what, until receiving Sabina's note, she must have considered to be a perfect crime.

"Do you always lock your office door when you're expecting a visitor?" The woman's voice was as icy as her appearance.

"Only when the visitor is a murderess."

"That is an abominable accusation. I could very easily sue you for defamation of character."

"You could if the accusation were false, which it isn't."

"Of course it is. Utterly false, utterly preposterous."

"Then why are you here? Why didn't you take my note to Harold Stennett or another attorney? Or to Lieutenant McGinn?"

Octavia Fairchild's chill gaze roamed the office, much as her husband's had on his visit; her rouged lip curled upward far enough to expose her gums. "What a nasty hovel this is. Exactly the sort of place I expected."

"You haven't answered my questions, Mrs. Fairchild. Why didn't you take my note to an attorney or the police, instead of coming here as directed?"

"I intend to do both after I've heard what evidence you claim to have against me. And I expect to make an additional charge."

"Oh? What would that be?"

"Attempted blackmail."

"Is that what you think? That I intend to blackmail you?"

"Why else would you have arranged this meeting? How much do you want?"

"How much will you pay?"

"Not one penny. I won't be blackmailed and I won't be bluffed."

"I am not bluffing. Why would I?"

"Then why haven't *you* gone to the police with this evidence of yours, if it's so damning?"

"Do you think I won't?"

"That is precisely what I think. You won't because you haven't any evidence, you couldn't possibly have because none exists."

"Oh, but it does. One piece, in fact, is in your possession."

"What do you mean by that?"

"The murder weapon, of course—your husband's hound's head walking stick."

The statement caused a slight eye-widening, a twitch at one corner of the rouged mouth—the first thin cracks in the ice mask. Sabina smiled and went to her desk. Octavia Fairchild remained standing, her hands thrust into the pockets of her muskrat coat.

"You felt no need to dispose of it, once it was cleaned of all traces of blood and other matter," Sabina went on when she was seated. "Even if you had, it would not have been as easy to spirit away as whatever bloodstained garment you wore. You might have concealed the stick under that coat you're wearing, but a stick is a cumbersome object that might well be noticed. No, it's still among your husband's effects at the hotel."

"Yes, it is. Clean and polished, as Roland always kept it. It could hardly be proven to have been used as a weapon."

"But it can. The wounds on his skull were made by its distinctive elongated knob and can be matched to it."

". . . How do you know that? The body was gone when you were brought to the room."

Sabina smiled again. "Detectives have ways of finding out such things."

"A match would hardly prove a case against me. The stick Charles used to murder Roland had a similar type of knob."

"No, it didn't. He carried his usual round-knobbed black-thorn stick when he paid his visit yesterday morning."

"You can't know that unless you've seen him, talked to him. You're harboring a murderer—"

"On the contrary, I'm conversing with one."

"It's Charles's word against mine. Whom do you suppose the police will believe, a bereaved widow or a madman who masquerades as Sherlock Holmes?"

"His, if corroborated by mine and by the rest of the case against you. Your motive, for instance."

"What motive could I possibly have?"

"The age-old one—wealth. With your husband dead and Charles the Third judged insane and incarcerated in an asylum, you stand to inherit the Fairchild millions as next of kin by marriage. You planned all along to dispose of Roland and frame his cousin for the crime. That is why you traveled to San Francisco with your husband, why you were so insistent that Charles be located and induced to meet privately with him."

"Conjecture. Sheer conjecture."

"When Charles left your hotel room yesterday, you picked up Roland's stick, brained him with it, then changed clothing and began screaming to attract attention. That is the way it happened, isn't it?"

"More ridiculous conjecture. You have no proof of any of this!"

"You're forgetting the gash on your cheek."

"What about it? It came from Charles's stick when he attacked me."

"No, it didn't. He never attacked you. It was your husband who gashed your cheek in an effort to ward off your attack on him."

"A scurrilous lie—"

"A fact, a provable fact. He inflicted the wound with two downward-hooked fingers on his right hand. You neglected to clean the skin and blood from beneath the nails on those two fingers. They're still there and can be matched to the gash."

Fissures had formed in the ice mask now. Even the eyes were no longer a glacial blue. The woman's fury had shifted from cold to hot, an inner fire that was melting the exterior chill.

"So you see, Mrs. Fairchild?" Sabina said. "That one fact alone is sufficient to cast serious doubt on the validity of your story. Combined with my testimony and that of the man you sought to frame, you stand no chance of getting away with your crime."

"The police . . . do they know any of this yet?"

"No, but they soon will."

"Have you told anyone else?"

"Only Charles."

"No one will pay heed to him."

"But the police will pay heed to me. I guarantee it. Why maintain your pretense of innocence? Why not admit the truth?"

More of the ice melted; the blue eyes held a fiery glow now.

"Damn you, why don't you drop *your* pretense. How much do you want to keep silent? Ten thousand dollars?"

Sabina shook her head.

"Twenty thousand? Fifty?"

"You couldn't buy my silence for ten times fifty thousand dollars. I can't be bought, Mrs. Fairchild. Your only hope is to admit the truth. To me, to Lieutenant McGinn. Admit that you murdered your husband. Admit your guilt."

All the ice was gone now; the woman's face was contorted with a feverish rage.

"Admit it," Sabina said relentlessly. "Admit that you bashed his brains in with his own stick. Admit—"

"All right! Yes! I killed him, I bashed his brains in and I'm glad of it! He was a failure and a cheat and a bully and I loathed him!"

The eruptive confession brought Sabina halfway out of her chair. But her elation turned to sudden dismay, for Octavia Fairchild had withdrawn a small-caliber pistol from her coat pocket.

Sight of the steadily pointed weapon froze Sabina. She could have kicked herself for not anticipating the possibility that Octavia Fairchild might have come here armed. Both her hands were clutching the desk edge; she let the right one slide off slowly, move downward to the partially open middle drawer.

"But you'll never tell anyone!" the woman cried. "You'll be as dead as Roland and no one will believe that lunatic Charles!"

Sabina's heart skipped a beat as her fingers touched the Remington derringer. Could she draw and fire it in time to save her life?

She was never to know the answer. For in that moment, the

alcove door flew open and out, bless him, came that lunatic Charles.

What happened next came so swiftly that it was almost a blur. He entered the office in a rush, his blackthorn stick upraised and flicking the air. Octavia Fairchild swung toward him, but she had no time to fire her pistol. In two slashing strokes Charles disarmed her: the first smacked her wrist and elicited a sharp cry of pain, the second, driven up underneath, popped the pistol free of her grasp and into an arc that allowed him to catch it deftly in midair with his free hand.

"Lunatic, indeed!" he snapped indignantly. "Charles, indeed! Holmes is the name, Sherlock Holmes, acknowledged expert at singlestick"—he waggled the blackthorn for emphasis—"as well as the use of sword, riding crop, and *baritsu.*"

Sabina sank down into her chair; she had faced a handgun twice before in her years as a detective, but in neither instance had she come so close to being shot, and her knees were understandably a little shaky. Edward Boone, who had also emerged from the alcove, stood gawping at Charles. So did Octavia Fairchild, clutching her wrist and grimacing in pain, but only for a few seconds. Then, all at once, she melted completely. Collapsed to the floor and puddled there, her face buried in her arms, tears of self-pity staining the sleeves of her brand-new muskrat coat.

"Now then," Sherlock Holmes said, "I will summon the police and finis will be written to, as the good Doctor Watson might have it, the Adventure of the Wronged Detective."

24

QUINCANNON

It was evening when he returned to the city. His arrival at the Ferry House would have been much later if he hadn't been fortunate in boarding the last southbound train just as it was leaving Los Alegres and then the ferry just as it was departing Sausalito.

He'd had plenty of time on the trip to decide on a way to accomplish the final phase of his mission. The one he settled on required immediate action, which meant postponing the night's rest his body craved after the long, wearying day. It also required breaking of the law (though only technically, in his view), and its success depended on his powers of persuasion and a not inconsiderable amount of luck. The risk bothered him not at all—he didn't exactly thrive on danger, but neither did he shy away from it—and it was the only method of recovering the stolen steam beer formula that did not involve violence. Besides which, if it could be accomplished it would provide an added element of satisfaction to the closing of the Golden State case.

Outside the Ferry House he boarded a Market Street trolley

and rode it to Fourteenth Street. From there he walked three blocks and turned onto Capp, a narrow residential street that contained facing rows of modest Victorian Stick-style houses. Light showed in the front windows of the fifth in the row on the south side. This one had been occupied by Slick Fingers Sam Rigsby and his wife for the past dozen or so years—except, that was, for the three years Slick Fingers had spent in Folsom Prison. It had been more than twelve months since Quincannon had had any contact with the man; if providence was with him, the Rigsbys would still be in residence.

It was and they were. The door was opened in answer to his turn of the bell by Anna Rigsby, a middle-aged harridan with the face of a dyspeptic mule and a disposition to match. Her mouth pinched into a lemony pucker when she recognized him. Her obvious dislike stemmed from the fact that Quincannon had been responsible for the three years her husband had spent as a guest of the state. Slick Fingers, on the other hand, held no grudge. Quincannon had spoken on his behalf at his trial, requesting leniency because Rigsby had been coerced by his two partners into taking part in the abortive bank caper, and as a result the judge had imposed the minimum sentence.

"Oh, it's you, is it," she said. "Don't tell me you're here to arrest Rigsby again?"

"On the contrary. Is he home?"

"What do you want with him?"

"A private conversation on a matter beneficial to both of us."

"Hah. Double-talk. Say it out plain or you don't come in."

"An offer of money—a sizable sum if he accepts a proposition I have for him. Plain enough?"

Her eyes took on an avaricious glitter. "Plain enough," she

said, and stood aside. Then, when Quincannon had entered the vestibule, "He's in the back bedroom working on another of his fool gadgets. Down the hall there, second door on the right."

The house smelled of a none-too-pleasant blend of boiled cabbage, cooked fish, dust, and dry rot. Mouth-breathing, he went along the hallway, the floorboards creaking ominously under his weight. The second door on the right stood ajar; he pushed it inward and stepped through.

"Good evening, Slick Fingers."

Rigsby was seated at a table on which was spread an array of tools, a soldering iron, metal rods and plates of various sizes, and other objects which Quincannon neither could nor cared to identify. Slick Fingers, in addition to his primary source of income, fancied himself an inventor. He tinkered continually with this or that mysterious contraption, none of which, so far as Quincannon knew, had ever earned him a dime.

He looked up, registered startlement and flickers of anxiety, started to stand, changed his mind, and sighed gustily as he sank back in his chair. A slender gent of some fifty hard-lived years, he had two distinguishing features: protuberant jumbo ears and large hands with long, spatulate fingers, both of which figured prominently in the plying of his chosen trade. He regarded Quincannon in a wary, defeated way, the expression of a man expecting to hear the voice of doom.

"I ain't done nothing," he said, his nervousness and his shifty gaze belying the words. "No box jobs since I got out of Folsom. I learned my lesson, I'm out of the game for good. Handyman work now when I can get it, that's all until I sell one of my inventions. Clean as a whistle."

"You needn't try to snow me. Once a box man, always a box man. And still the best in the business, I'll wager."

Slick Fingers almost but not quite managed to conceal his pride at the compliment. "What is it you want, Mr. Quincannon?"

Quincannon shut the door behind him before he answered. "Your expertise and a few hours of your time, in order to right a wrong. For which you'll be well paid."

"I don't see what— Wait a minute. You ain't here to offer me a box job?"

"That's precisely why I'm here."

"What kind? Legit?"

"Not exactly."

"You mean you want me to crack a safe and *steal* what's in it?"

"Something in it, yes."

Slick Fingers shook his head, as if the proposition had rattled his senses. "Geez," he said, "I never figured you for a thief."

Quincannon winced, recalling his righteous thought in Caleb Lansing's rooms that he was many things but a thief wasn't one of them. "Extenuating circumstances demand it," he said, as much in self-defense as explanation to Rigsby. A man was not a thief, after all, if he had no intention of realizing illegal profits from the commission of an unlawful act.

"What is it you want swiped?"

"One or two pieces of paper." Assuming the formula was still in Cyrus Drinkwater's office safe, but the odds were good that it was. The old reprobate had no real cause yet to have moved it elsewhere, nor to have had it copied. Though he might well do one or both when he got wind of Elias Corby's arrest. Immediate action, therefore, was imperative.

"No money or other valuables?"

"Just the paper or papers, nothing more."

"You mind if I ask why?"

"I told you. To right a wrong."

"No, I mean why you picked me for the job?"

"Because you're the best box man in California. And a close-mouthed fellow when a job's done and a proper price paid for it."

The same sort of avarice that had been in his wife's eyes sparked the cracksman's. "How much?"

"Two hundred and fifty dollars," Quincannon said. He could afford to be generous; James Willard would be the one to foot the bill.

The figure made Slick Fingers suck in his breath. "That's a lot of lettuce. You must want them papers pretty bad."

"I do, in order to close a case. Well? Is the fee enough to put you back in the game?"

"I dunno, I got to think about it. What kind of box is it?"

"I don't know."

"You don't know? Well, Jesus, Mr. Quincannon . . ."

"Does it matter? You've been known to brag that there's not a safe made you can't crack."

"Yeah, sure, that's true," Slick Fingers said. "But I got to have some idea what I'm dealing with. If it's one of these so-called burglarproof boxes they're manufacturing nowadays, likely you got to blow the door to open it up. That takes a lot of work. And I don't work with soup, you know that."

"I wouldn't want it blown open no matter what kind it is.

Given the location, this job has to be done with as little noise as possible. And without damage to the safe."

"What's the location?"

"An office in a building near Civic Center."

"Whoa." Slick Fingers held up both hands, palms outward. "Office building, Civic Center . . . public places like that are too hard to get into."

"Not for me."

"You mean you got a key?"

"I don't need a key. I'll have no trouble getting us in."

"Us? You'd be there, too?"

"The entire time," Quincannon said. "Inside the building, inside the office. All you have to do is open the safe."

"If I can." Rigsby scratched his long fingers through the remaining few strands of hair clinging to his scalp. Then he said musingly, half to himself, "Downtown office . . . so it won't be an old box, the kind you can crack with a hammer. A hammer's out anyway . . . no noise, no damage. Won't need to take my kit, just a dark lantern and a stethoscope, and hope it's a box with a rotary combination dial."

A cracksman's kit, Quincannon knew, was a small valise packed with a carpenter's hand brace, the drill bits known as "dan" and "stems," a ball-peen hammer, and a pinch bar, among other items. He said, "Most safes have rotary combination dials, don't they?"

"Most."

"Then chances are this one will, too. And opening one of that type by ear and touch is your specialty. Slick Fingers Sam Rigsby, the best lock manipulator in the state."

"Hell, in the entire West."

"Are you in, then?"

"When's the job to be?"

"Tonight. Late."

"Tonight! Does it have to be so soon?"

"Yes. There's no time to waste."

Slick Fingers ruminated in silence for a clutch of seconds. Then he said, "Suppose the box is one I can't crack by taking the high road." Meaning his specialty method of lock manipulation; the use of tools and brute strength was considered the "low road" in safecracking. "Do I still get the two-fifty?"

"You do."

"Guaranteed? Word of honor?"

"Guaranteed. Word of honor."

The promise made up the cracksman's mind for him. "All right, Mr. Quincannon," he said. "You talked me into it. I just hope I ain't gonna live to regret it."

So did Quincannon.

Three A.M.

Neither vehicle nor pedestrian was abroad on the block of Turk Street where Cyrus Drinkwater's office was located. A sharp night wind blew scraps of paper like will-o'-the-wisps along the empty passage. Electroliers cut pale strips of light out of the darkness, but the puddles of illumination on the cobblestones and sidewalks only deepened the shadows around them. All the windows in the two-story brick building were dark. Those in Drinkwater's office above appeared to be curtained or blinded, though Quincannon couldn't be absolutely sure from street level.

He went to work on the door latch with his lock picks, Slick Fingers beside him in the doorway keeping watch for a beat patrolman or anyone else who might happen along. No one did in the two minutes it took Quincannon to snap the last of the tumblers into place. He opened the door, led the way quickly inside the small lobby.

There was a single elevator, he recalled, in the left-hand wall and a staircase at the rear. He flicked a lucifer alight with his thumbnail, shielding the flare with his other hand, and used it to guide the way to the stairs before blowing it out. They climbed to the second floor in total blackness. Once there, he whispered, "To the right," and turned in that direction, Slick Fingers close behind him. Drinkwater's office, one of six in the building, took up the far right-hand corner, its windows overlooking both Turk and Hyde.

A few strides clear of the stairs, Quincannon halted and fired another match, again shielding the glow with his free hand. "Light your lantern here," he said.

Rigsby went to one knee, took the small dark lantern from under his coat, and opened the shutter. Quincannon quickly lit the wick, shook out the lucifer as Slick Fingers lowered the shutter again—not quite all the way, allowing a sliver of a beam. By its glow they went ahead to Drinkwater's door.

It took Quincannon even less time to pick the lock here. Before they entered, Rigsby completely shuttered the lantern's eye. The darkness inside the outer office was complete, which meant that the windows were fully covered. He said as much to Slick Fingers, who then reopened the lantern to a slit.

The safe was not in this room; Quincannon would have noticed it on his previous visit if it were. The door to Drinkwater's private sanctum was to the left, beyond a rail divider and his secretary's desk. It wasn't locked. Again, before entering, Slick Fingers extinguished his light—a precaution that once more proved to be unnecessary. The Hyde Street windows were also covered. Drinkwater had a fetish for the color maroon; the drapes and deep pile carpet were all of that dark red shade.

The safe was not positioned in plain view, but it took Rigsby, whose long experience had given him a sixth sense not unlike that of a hound on the scent, less than a minute to locate it—hidden behind a pair of doors beneath shelves on the wall next to a massive cherrywood desk. He opened the lantern's eye halfway in order to examine it. It had a rotary dial, Quincannon was relieved to see. Slick Fingers peered at the manufacturer's name in gold leaf on its black-painted front, then rotated the dial several times before turning his head and offering up a snaggle-toothed grin.

"Piece of cake," he said.

Quincannon watched him take a doctor's stethoscope from the pocket of his coat, fit the earpieces into his jumbo ears, place the chestpiece against the safe door just above the dial, and then set to work. Lock manipulation was a simple enough process in principle: the lock was used against itself in order to discover the combination, by feel and by the sound of the tumblers falling into place in proper sequence as the dial was slowly rotated. But it took a highly skilled cracksman with a clear understanding of the mechanical actions of locks, plus years of practice, to do the job properly and swiftly.

It took Slick Fingers less than fifteen minutes to crack this box. In his high-road world, the job had indeed been a piece of cake.

As soon as he had the door open, Quincannon knelt beside him and began to sift through the contents. The safe contained all sorts of documents, a banded packet of greenbacks—and in an unmarked manila envelope, two pages of hen-scratch jottings that were clearly the ingredients and measurements for the manufacture of steam beer.

"That what you're after, Mr. Quincannon?"

"It is."

Slick Fingers looked longingly at the sheaf of greenbacks. "Sure there's nothing else you want?"

"I'm sure. Close the safe now and we'll be on our way."

They encountered no trouble leaving the building or the neighborhood. On Market Street, before they parted to take early-morning trolleys in opposite directions, Quincannon reassured Rigsby that he would be paid his $250 on the morrow, and made the cracksman even happier by adding that he would also receive a bonus for a job well done. With Otto Ackermann's recipe safely in his possession, Quincannon could afford—or rather, James Willard could afford—to be magnanimous.

On his way home for a few hours of much-needed sleep, Quincannon's spirits were high. The irony in tonight's successful mission was a pleasure to contemplate. He might not be able to prove that Cyrus Drinkwater was behind the original theft of the recipe, but once the old scoundrel discovered it was missing from his safe, neither would he be able to prove that Quincannon was responsible. Ordinarily such a potential stalemate would have meant the job he'd been hired to do was left unfinished. Not so in this case. He had solved the murders of Otto Ackermann and Caleb Lansing, ranged far in order to yaffle the perpetrator, and recovered the stolen property which he would soon place in James Willard's hands.

No detective could have done more to satisfy his client, earn his fee, and serve the interests of justice.

25

SABINA

The envelope was mixed in with several others that had been pushed through the slot in the agency door. But it had not been delivered by the postman; it bore no stamp or address, only Sabina's name. The penmanship told her immediately whom it was from.

At her desk she slit open the envelope. Inside were two sheets of good-quality vellum paper, both completely filled with writing in the same familiar Spencerian hand.

My dear Mrs. Carpenter:
I must apologize for my failure to return after summoning the police yesterday, thus leaving you and Mr. Boone the task of rendering explanations. You may have considered my disappearance, as it were, to be a cowardly act, and in a sense so it was. However, I simply could not countenance a long interrogation in which my lineage would have yet again been

questioned by police officials and representatives of the legal profession. The possibility that I might be forcibly shipped off to Chicago and entangled in a pointless legal rumpus over the estate of a stranger was also a factor in my decision. Protection of both my good name and my good works must take precedence over all other considerations.

For the same reason, I have concluded that I must with all dispatch finally take my leave of your fair city. The publicity I have received regarding this odious Fairchild affair, as well as that of the incident at the Rayburn Gallery, makes it extremely difficult if not impossible to continue my private inquiries here. By the time you receive this missive, I shall have pulled up stakes, as you Americans so quaintly put it, and sped upon my way.

I do not yet know my next destination. Perhaps I shall return directly to England and my Baker Street lodgings, put the good Doctor Watson's mind at rest as to my welfare, and openly resume my practice as a consulting detective. On the other hand, perhaps I shall take up temporary residence in another American city (though not, of course, Chicago), or in a European metropolis such as Paris or Vienna.

My only regret in leaving so precipitately is that I cannot inform you of my decision, gaze one last time upon your charming personage, and bid you adieu in person. Perhaps this letter, too, is an act of cowardice, but it nonetheless prevents any attempt on your part to dissuade me, as well as any recriminations and tears. We must both console ourselves with the possibility, however remote at this point in time, that I will return to San Francisco one day in future and have the distinct pleasure of once again joining forces with you and the estimable Mr. Quincannon.

Until that day, should it ever come, I wish you continued success in our shared and noble profession, good health, and safe passage wherever you may go.

With respect and admiration,

Your obedient servant,

S. Holmes, Esq.

Sabina set the letter down. Tears! As if she would shed even one over the sudden departure of a delusional individual who was neither British nor a famous detective. Or console herself with the thought that she might be subjected to his interfering ways again! The unmitigated gall of the man, making such ridiculous statements after having left her to the none-too-tender mercies of Lieutenant McGinn and stuffy Harold Stennett, who had been summoned to act on behalf of the Fairchild family's attorneys, in order to pull the addlepate's chestnuts out of the fire. She was glad he was gone, glad he would never again pop up unexpectedly at some inopportune time to make her life and her work more difficult with his foolish disguises, his insufferable ego.

And yet—

And yet there was no gainsaying the fact that he also possessed a number of laudable qualities. He'd saved her from being shot by the wild-eyed Octavia Fairchild, hadn't he? And always treated her in a cordial, even courtly fashion, with as much respect for her sleuthing abilities as his assumed Sherlockian arrogance would allow—more respect than McGinn and Stennett had demonstrated, certainly. And brought her the kitten Eve as a companion for Adam. And helped her and John solve more than one difficult case . . .

Oh, drat! The truth was she didn't know quite how she felt about Charles Percival Fairchild III, whether she liked or disliked him, whether she was more delighted or more sorry to have him gone from her life, and the ambivalence was bothersome in the extreme. Appropriately enough, given his tendency to be bothersome in the extreme.

One thing she did know for certain: John would be ecstatic when he learned that the aggravating thorn in his side had finally removed itself. He had never forgiven S. Holmes, Esquire, for providing much of the solution to the Bughouse Affair, thereby stealing his thunder. At times his ego could become as inflated as that of his nemesis, though it never quite swelled to an objectionable degree.

And where *was* John? He hadn't been to the agency in three days now, nor left her any kind of message to explain his absence. Sabina had begun to feel pricklings of concern. If anything had happened to him . . .

Nothing had. Her fears were alleviated shortly past eleven-thirty when he burst into the office, rather like a bewhiskered bull entering a china shop, waving a handful of newspapers and looking both vexed and bleary-eyed. "I've just seen these!" he half shouted. "What in heaven's name have you been getting yourself into?"

"Nothing I couldn't get myself out of," she said calmly, managing to conceal her relief that he was unharmed. "As the accounts in those sheets plainly state."

"Not the one by Homer Keeps in last night's *Evening Bulletin*. He as much as accuses you of harboring a fugitive lunatic."

"A pox on Homer Keeps. The Fairchild misadventure has been satisfactorily resolved."

"Charles Percival Fairchild the Third. An appropriate moniker for a crackbrain. Heir to a Chicago manufacturer's fortune . . . bah! Why didn't you tell me you'd been hired to track him down?"

"You know the answer to that, John, given the way you feel about the man."

"How did you find him? Why did you let him involve you in two crimes in two days including a homicide? There's little enough in these rags to explain any of that."

"It's a long story. Sit down and I'll recount it to you."

"I haven't time now for a long story. I'm on my way to pay a debt and to deliver the stolen steam beer formula to James Willard."

"But when you saw the newspaper headlines you had to rush

up here to chastise me and make sure I haven't gotten into any more trouble."

"No, no. To make sure you're all right, and to find out what the devil—"

"I'm fine, and so, I see, are you. I take it you've wrapped up the Golden State case?"

"I have. Yes. Naturally."

"Very well, then," Sabina said. "We can regale each other with our triumphs later. For now, suffice it to say that neither of us will have any more trouble with Charles Fairchild the Third, alias Sherlock Holmes. As a result of all the publicity, he has left San Francisco with no intention of returning."

"He has? Are you sure?"

"Positive."

That mollified John enough to put an end to his fulminating. His only remark, at least for the present, was a relatively mild, "Good riddance to the blasted nuisance."

When he was gone, Sabina reread Charles's letter. *Good riddance, nuisance?* she thought when she laid it down again. *Or good-bye, comrade?*

26

"A plague of thieves," Quincannon said.

Sabina looked at him questioningly.

"That is what you and I have been dealing with the past several days. You with the Fairchild woman and the crafty pincher from Sacramento and his brother-in-law at the Rayburn Gallery. And I with Lansing, Corby, Jones, and Cyrus Drinkwater." He might have added his name and that of Slick Fingers Sam Rigsby to the list, though of course he didn't; their nocturnal escapade in Drinkwater's office would remain his secret, thus sparing him Sabina's disapproval. "Thieves, the lot of them. A plague of thieves."

"I hadn't thought of it that way, but of course you're right. We were fortunate to have brought them all to justice."

"Not quite all. Drinkwater is still free as a bird, at least for the nonce. But if I have my way, he'll pay for this and his other crimes one day."

They had just been seated in an intimate booth in the Tadich Grill, a landmark establishment known as San Francisco's "Cold Day" restaurant. The appellation had nothing to do with the city's weather; it stemmed from a boast a politician named Alexander Badham had made there, to the effect that it would be a cold day when he was defeated for reelection, shortly before he was soundly trounced at the polls. Both Quincannon and Sabina wore evening clothes, for after dinner they would attend one of Charles Hoyt's farcical sketches at the New Bush Theater. Quincannon had no particular liking for drawing room comedies, but since Sabina did he was perfectly willing to accommodate her—in this and anything else on their social evenings together. And with no ulterior motives in mind. The pleasure of her company and the prospect of more evenings to come were satisfaction enough.

He favored her with a toothsome smile. She had dressed well for him tonight, as he had for her in his best tailcoat suit, a light-colored waistcoat, and a white tie. Her gown was of ruby-red brocade with a lace-trimmed bodice and a fluffy, floor-length skirt. Pendant ruby earrings, a wedding gift from her late husband, made a fiery complement to her sleek dark hair. Even more to his liking was the shell brooch at her breast—a gift from her doting partner and would-be swain the previous Christmas.

She allowed him to openly admire her without comment. As a matter of fact, unless he was very much mistaken, she seemed to bask in his attention, something she had never done in the offices of Carpenter and Quincannon, Professional Detective Services, and only to a minimal degree on their previous social engagements. She truly did seem to be weakening toward him, he thought. No, "weakening" was the wrong word. Mellowing. Returning his affection in kind, if still a bit warily.

A waiter brought their libations, a glass of Chablis for her and a cup of warm clam juice for him, and took their dinner selections. Sabina opted for crab cakes, Quincannon for the oyster and bacon frittata known as Hangtown Fry, both Tadich specialties.

When the waiter departed, they toasted each other's good health. After which Sabina said, "You know, John, there's one thing about the murder of Caleb Lansing you neglected to explain to me. Not on purpose, I trust."

"I would never knowingly withhold pertinent information from you, my dear." A prevarication, but a harmless one. "If I neglected to explain something, it was purely an oversight. What was it?"

"How Elias Corby managed his escape from the brewery's utility room and storeroom. Usually you trumpet your clever deductions."

"Trumpet? Well . . . perhaps. I did tell you about my discovery of the lupulin, didn't I?"

"The powder residue from freshly picked hop flowers, yes, and how you found it in both the storeroom and Corby's office. But not how he was able to miraculously escape from two locked rooms."

"I must have been distracted in some way or other . . . Ah, the telephone. It rang while I was finishing up my account and you spent several minutes talking with our new client, Mr. Friedlander."

"Yes, and we were both so eager to discuss his troubles that we failed to continue with the Corby matter. I only realized it as I was dressing earlier tonight."

Quincannon hadn't realized it at all until she'd brought it

up—the result, no doubt, of the prospect of a substantial fee from a land baron as wealthy as J. M. Friedlander. Still, he was surprised at himself. Ordinarily he derived considerable pleasure from elucidating the details of one of his deductions. And would again . . . now.

He fluffed his well-groomed whiskers and temporarily adopted a brisk professional air. "The dried lupulin was the essential clue," he said, "along with two others. The fact that Corby appeared in the storerooms so soon after we discovered Lansing's body. And the man's stature."

"What do you mean, his stature?"

"Just that. He was the only Golden State employee who could have been guilty."

Sabina nudged his ankle with the toe of her slipper. "Don't be cryptic, John. Please get to the point before the food arrives. You know I dislike discussing business while dining."

"The short and sweet of it, then. Once Corby fired the fatal shot, for the reasons I outlined previously—self-protection and Lansing's share of the money from the theft of the formula— he placed the revolver near Lansing's hand and rifled his pocket for the storeroom key. In different circumstances he would have simply unlocked the storeroom door and slipped out at the first opportunity. But he'd heard the sounds I made at the door, knew the shot had been heard and the passage was blocked and he was therefore trapped there with a dead man. What could he do?"

"Well? What did he do?"

"He had two options," Quincannon said. "Hold fast and bluff it out, claim that he'd tried and failed to stop Lansing from shooting himself. But he had no way of knowing how much I knew and must have feared that such a story would not be believed. His second option was to hide and hope his hiding place would be overlooked in the first rush.

"Corby was quick-witted, I'll give him that. He had less than five minutes to formulate and implement his plan and he must have used every second. His first act would have been to lock the utility room door; the key that operates the storeroom door lock works on that one as well. The purpose being to create more confusion and solidify the impression that Lansing had committed suicide. He then entered the room containing the sacks of malt and hops and established his hiding place."

"Where?" Sabina asked. "You said you looked into that room immediately after the door was unlocked and there was no place for a man to hide."

"No obvious place. Corby counted on the fact that the first inspection would be cursory, and he was quite right, it was. If there had been time for a careful search then, I would have found him quickly enough. But I and the others were intent on finding out what had happened to Lansing."

"Well? Where was he?"

"When I first looked into the storage area, I registered a single sack of hops propped against the end wall. When I returned later, the sack was no longer there; it had been moved back into the tightly wedged row along the side wall. That and the pile of empty sacks gave me the answer."

"Ah! Corby hid *inside* one of the empty sacks."

"Just so," Quincannon said. "He dragged a full sack from the end of the row, climbed into an empty one or pulled it down over him, and wedged himself into the space. When he heard the locked door being opened and the group of us rushing in, he held himself in such a motionless position that he resembled the other sacks in the row. Now you see what I meant by his stature being an essential clue to his guilt. Only a pint-sized man could have fit inside a fifty-pound hop sack."

"And while you and the other men were huddled around Lansing's body, Corby quickly stepped out of the sack, replaced it on the pile of empties, returned the full sack to its proper place, and pretended to have just arrived."

"Precisely. It struck me as odd at the time that he should have shown up when and where he did. A brewery's bookkeeper has little business in the storerooms."

"The lupulin you found in his office came from the hideout sack?"

"From inside it, yes. Residue clung to the twill of his trousers and perhaps inside the cuffs. Golden State buys its hops from a farm in Oregon's Willamette Valley. The flowers are picked, dried, and sacked there, and now and then dried hops are put into bags previously used by pickers. In such cases, a residue of the yellow powder clings to the interior of the burlap."

"Well done, John, I must say. Your usual excellent detective work."

"No more so," Quincannon said magnanimously, "than yours in uncovering the hiding place of the stolen Marie Antoinette handbag."

They smiled at each other across the candlelit table.

The arrival of their dinners broke the pleasant spell of the moment. The food was superb, as always at the Tadich Grill, and they spoke little as they tucked into it. Quincannon finished his Hangtown Fry in short order and was in the process of loading his briar from his oilskin pouch when he saw that Sabina had paused and was gazing off into the middle distance, an oddly wistful expression on her face.

"What are you thinking about, my dear?"

"Oh," she said, blinking and focusing on him again, "I couldn't help wondering if we would ever see Charles the Third again."

Quincannon repressed a scowl. "If the pompous rattlepate knows what's good for him, he'll never again darken either of our doors."

"Yes, he's pompous, and meddlesome and annoying, but he can also be charming and helpful and . . . well, even endearing at times."

"Endearing! Faugh!"

"You're not forgetting, are you, that he saved my life?"

"Of course not. For that, he has my undying gratitude."

"That, if nothing else, endears him to me," Sabina said. "And you must admit that in spite of his clownish disguises and his addled ways, he really is a very good detective. The genuine Sherlock Holmes, even though it's his identity that has been usurped, might even have been proud of the manner in which Charles adroitly adopted his methods."

"By Jove, you sound as though you're going to miss him."

"In a curious way, I think I shall."

Quincannon stared at her as if she'd temporarily taken leave of her senses. She caught the look, smiled, and reached across the table to lay her hand on his. "Don't be jealous, John. Of course you're the better detective, by far."

At some other time he might have responded to her praise, but with her hand resting warmly on his in this intimate atmosphere he barely even heard the words. Her touch, the twining of her fingers around his, thrilled him. Impulsively he placed his other hand on top of hers, and when she made no move to end the joining, he applied a gentle squeeze which she then returned. This thrilled him even more, and not, by Godfrey, in a sexual way. All he felt in that moment was an acute and gentle tenderness, which, if her expression was a proper indicator, she was feeling as well.

At last, he thought.

Ah, at last!